Everlasting

The Queen's Alpha Series, Volume 2

W.J. May

Published by Dark Shadow Publishing, 2018.

EVERLASTING

First edition. February 1, 2018.

Written by W.J. May.

Also by W.J. May

Bit-Lit Series
Lost Vampire
Cost of Blood
Price of Death

Blood Red Series
Courage Runs Red
The Night Watch
Marked by Courage
Forever Night

Daughters of Darkness: Victoria's Journey
Victoria
Huntress
Coveted (A Vampire & Paranormal Romance)
Twisted

Hidden Secrets Saga

Seventh Mark - Part 1
Seventh Mark - Part 2
Marked By Destiny
Compelled
Fate's Intervention
Chosen Three
The Hidden Secrets Saga: The Complete Series

Paranormal Huntress Series
Never Look Back
Coven Master
Alpha's Permission

Prophecy Series
Only the Beginning
White Winter
Secrets of Destiny

The Chronicles of Kerrigan
Rae of Hope
Dark Nebula
House of Cards
Royal Tea
Under Fire
End in Sight
Hidden Darkness
Twisted Together
Mark of Fate

Strength & Power
Last One Standing
Rae of Light
The Chronicles of Kerrigan Box Set Books # 1 - 6

The Chronicles of Kerrigan: Gabriel
Living in the Past
Staring at the Future
Present For Today

The Chronicles of Kerrigan Prequel
Question the Darkness
Into the Darkness
Fight the Darkness
Alone in the Darkness
Lost in Darkness
Christmas Before the Magic
The Chronicles of Kerrigan Prequel Series Books #1-3

The Chronicles of Kerrigan Sequel
A Matter of Time
Time Piece
Second Chance
Glitch in Time
Our Time
Precious Time

The Hidden Secrets Saga
Seventh Mark (part 1 & 2)

The Queen's Alpha Series
Eternal
Everlasting
Unceasing

The Senseless Series
Radium Halos
Radium Halos - Part 2
Nonsense

Standalone
Shadow of Doubt (Part 1 & 2)
Five Shades of Fantasy
Shadow of Doubt - Part 1
Shadow of Doubt - Part 2
Four and a Half Shades of Fantasy
Dream Fighter
What Creeps in the Night
Forest of the Forbidden
Arcane Forest: A Fantasy Anthology
Ancient Blood of the Vampire and Werewolf

THE QUEEN'S ALPHA SERIES
EVERLASTING

USA TODAY BESTSELLING AUTHOR
W . J .   M A Y

THE QUEEN'S ALPHA SERIES

EVERLASTING

USA Today Bestselling Author

W. J. MAY

Have You Read the C.o.K Series?

The Chronicles of Kerrigan
Book I - *Rae of Hope* is FREE!

BOOK TRAILER:

http://www.youtube.com/watch?v=gILAwXxx8MU

How hard do you have to shake the family tree to find the truth about the past?

Fifteen year-old Rae Kerrigan never really knew her family's history. Her mother and father died when she was young and it is only when she accepts a scholarship to the prestigious Guilder Boarding School in England that a mysterious family secret is revealed.

Will the sins of the father be the sins of the daughter?

As Rae struggles with new friends, a new school and a star-struck forbidden love, she must also face the ultimate challenge: receive a tattoo on her sixteenth birthday with specific powers that may bind her to an unspeakable darkness. It's up to Rae to undo the dark evil in her family's past and have a ray of hope for her future.

Find W.J. May

Website:
http://www.wanitamay.yolasite.com
Facebook:
https://www.facebook.com/pages/Author-WJ-May-FAN-PAGE/
141170442608149
Newsletter:
SIGN UP FOR W.J. May's Newsletter to find out about new releases,
updates, cover reveals and even freebies!
http://eepurl.com/97aYf

EVERLASTING Blurb:

When the crown prince puts a bounty on her head, Katerina and her friends find themselves facing trouble at every turn. It's a race to get to the safe house in time, but will they pull together to work as a team, or will their differences pull them apart?

Strengths and weaknesses are put to the test as Katerina is plunged headfirst into a magical world she never knew existed. Fiction becomes reality as the characters from her childhood fairytales come to life, bringing with them secrets she could never have imagined.

Her bloodline gives her the right to call herself their queen, but is the division between the royal family and the magical kingdom too great? How can she mend the damage of the past?

More importantly...can she be the one to unite her people?

The Queen's Alpha Series

Eternal
Everlasting
Unceasing
Evermore
Forever

Chapter 1

"Dylan, is that you?"
The wolf met her eyes for a moment before dropping its head with yet another frustrated sigh. A sigh that Katerina had heard many times before. A sigh that promised a furious lecture soon to come.

There aren't many things you can utter when the guy you've been travelling around with for the last month and a half suddenly turns into a wolf. And he failed to tell you.

Katerina wracked her brain. Trying to come up with anything remotely appropriate.

She bypassed the standard exclamations of shock. The cheesy one-liners designed to hide her bug-eyed surprise. She even avoided all her defense-mechanistic jokes—resisting the urge to throw a large stick and see whether or not he would fetch it back. In the end, she opted for a strange sort of comradery. She'd held a secret from him—even though he'd known all along—but that wasn't the point. She thought about how he'd reacted when she told him she was the missing princess. A bizarre empathetic response she happened to think was both kind and comforting, while others, historically, did not. All this was running through her head as those blue eyes stared—or possibly glared—at her.

Tell him something about yourself. Something weird. Fair is fair.

Her confidence soared, and she was about to confide a story about how she, too, used to run around pretending to be a creature of the forest. Back with Kailas when they were both still children and he hadn't yet tried to kill her. But before she could get a chance to speak, the image in front of her changed.

A loud voice rang angrily through the clearing. "You STUPID girl!"

It turned out Dylan had enough words for them both.

Gone was the chocolate fur. Gone were the razor claws. Replaced instead with a guy so beside himself she'd be surprised if he didn't lift right off the ground. He didn't. He stormed across it instead. Coming to a stop just inches away from her.

Completely naked.

"What the heck were you thinking?!"

The birds cringed away from his voice. Taking to the skies and leaving the volatile scene in the little clearing far behind them. The princess was not so lucky.

"There was this kid," she started to say, although by now it seemed a rather transparent deception. "He was crying, and I was trying to—"

"I don't care about some KID!" Dylan thundered, completely oblivious to the rays of sunlight glinting off his bare chest. "WHAT did you DO?!"

She had wandered off. Left Tanya behind. Disobeyed his direct orders. The anger was understandable. His choice of words, however, was not.

"What did I *do*?" she repeated, trying her best to understand whilst forbidding her eyes to stray anywhere beneath his neck. There was enough going on right now without adding on the first naked body she'd ever seen. "I'm trying to tell you. Wait... What do you mean—"

"I couldn't track you!" he shouted, eyes wide and feral. "I couldn't find you!"

However impossible it seemed, she suddenly found herself more frightened than she'd been at any point during the fight. It was his voice that did it. And the look in his eyes.

She'd never seen this side of him. The loss of control. The panic. The only time she'd even seen him flustered was when they'd been in Bernie's cave; to be fair, he'd thought there was a legitimate chance he was about to be turned into soup.

Then all at once, it clicked.

"Alwyn's spell..." she murmured. Her eyes widened as they lifted to the forest trees, but before she could gather her thoughts she was abruptly grounded by that angry voice.

"What?"

Dylan had kept a firm hand on her ever since the paws had disappeared and he had hands to use. Even now, with both her attackers lying in pieces, he seemed incredibly reluctant to let go.

"I had a spell put on me when I left the palace," she was quick to explain. "A spell to make me impossible to track." Her eyes flickered down to his hand and her cheeks flushed with guilt. "It was supposed to have worn off by now. I didn't think—"

"No, you DIDN'T think!" he thundered. "You NEVER do!"

The words echoed violently among the trees, but even as he shouted them he pulled her closer. Searching her over for damages. Combing his fingers through her hair. Lifting her chin to check her eyes for a concussion. Running his hands along the base of her skull, the top of her collarbone. Down her arms and all the way to her wrists. It was there that he stopped. Breathing heavily. Holding her tight against his bare chest.

She closed her eyes and leaned against him. Trying to stop shaking. Taking a strange sort of comfort in the proximity, no matter how enraged he'd become.

"You just go wandering off in the woods, chasing after crying children. Picking fights with vampires. Stumbling upon giants and bands of assassins! No matter how many times I tell you not to! No matter how many times it comes back to BITE US IN THE ARSE!"

Katerina flinched, and her eyes filled with tears. In her periphery she saw Cassiel and Tanya rush into the clearing, weapons drawn. They took one look at the carnage and stopped short, staring warily at the couple standing in the middle of it all.

"Why should I have expected anything different from you?" Dylan released her in a single motion, spitting on the ground as he paced to the other side of the clearing. Little streams of crimson were dripping down his back, like he'd wandered out of some macabre portrait, but Katerina didn't think any of the blood was his. The only wounds Dylan had sustained in the fight were internal. Though he was doing his best to exorcise them now.

"Chasing after some kid..." He paced and cursed, muttering furiously to himself for another moment, before whirling back around and focusing all that rage on her. "It doesn't matter how many squirrels you eat, how many bogs you sleep in—you're just a stupid, spoiled little princess."

Their eyes met and something between them died.

"That's all you'll ever be." He stormed away without another word. Without a glance behind him. Without addressing the fact that he still wasn't wearing any pants. He left Katerina standing behind him, feeling like a hole had been stabbed right through her chest. If he'd used a blade, it couldn't have cut any deeper.

...because he's right.

A feeling of hopelessness settled over her. One that had very little to do with the attack, and far more to do with the reprimand afterwards. She'd been expecting some degree of sympathy. A hint of concern. Or perhaps even a casual explanation for how the hell the man she'd been travelling around with had suddenly turned into a giant dog.

What she hadn't expected was the truth. But Dylan Aires didn't shy away from the truth.

It didn't matter how hard she tried to fit in. It didn't matter what skills she learned, or what sacrifices she made, or what lengths she'd gone to adjust to her new reality.

She was just a princess. A scared, sheltered little princess whose tragic naivety was bound to get either herself or someone around her killed.

Tanya would never have wandered off like that. Cassiel would never have believed the boy. Dylan would have been able to defend himself. What the heck was I thinking?

She didn't know how long she stood there. It must have been a while, because some of the birds had ventured back to their overhead perch by the time Tanya placed a sudden hand on her shoulder. Katerina jumped, then glanced over in surprise. She'd almost forgotten the others were still standing there. Waiting. Just as she realized she was waiting herself.

The shifter flashed her a sympathetic smile, gazed out towards the trees, then broached the subject with all the grace of a battering ram. "So...he can turn into a wolf, huh?"

IF THE MORNING HAD started badly, the rest of the day wasn't looking to be any better.

The booze and medical supplies were wrapped in blankets and tucked safely into Tanya's pack. The rooms were closed out, and the bar tabs were settled. They hit the forest trail an hour later than expected and started moving at a near frantic place to make up the lost time. According to the men, who had apparently made the journey before, it was a virtual nightmare. The more ground they could cover each day, the better chance they stood.

But it wasn't the logistics that had Katerina concerned. It wasn't the grueling pace, or the treacherous journey, or the fact that it seemed frightfully cold for the middle of summer.

Dylan didn't speak to her. Not a single word. For the next *eleven* hours.

At first, it was scary. Then it became depressing. Then it grew almost impressive as hour eleven stretched into hour twelve. The man may have come from nothing, but he'd certainly mastered the art of holding a grudge. No matter how many times Katerina tried to catch his attention, he kept his eyes locked firmly on the horizon. No matter how many times she tried to prompt him with a soft question or a quiet observation, he acted as though she wasn't even there. When she tripped over a log and went tumbling down the side of a ravine, he motioned to Tanya to help.

The sun rose and fell in the sky but, still, not a single word.

At first, the deafening silence was hard to ignore. But by the time they stopped for the night to pitch the tent and start a fire, Katerina found herself welcoming the quiet. At the very least, it gave her a chance to think. From the second she'd seen the wolf, standing in all his majestic glory, a dozen little things had started clicking into place.

The fact that he was able to hear more than he should. The fact that he was able to see more than he should. The fact that he recognized the pack of wolf shifters down by the wagons.

Everything, right down to that effortless grace with which he carried himself, spoke to being blessed with some otherworldly power. In a way, she was surprised she hadn't guessed it sooner.

That's why he hugged me, that day on the road. It wasn't affection; he was learning my scent.

She remembered it like it was yesterday. The way she'd scampered down the hill, wearing her new dress. The way he'd walked out to meet her, pulling her in for an unexpected embrace. The way his hands lingered on her clothing, his face brushed against her hair...

But why didn't he tell me? Her mind wandered as she tossed down another handful of kindling for the fire. *Why didn't he just tell me he was a shifter? Why keep it some big secret?*

In spite of her best intentions, Alwyn's final words of warning echoed sharply through her head. 'Never trust a shifter. They are loyal to the crown.' Her eyes flickered up to Dylan, settling a moment on his handsome face. Well, he certainly didn't have any love for the crown, but he *was* a shifter. And she was trusting him with her very life. What would her old mentor think about that?

"Nice face."

They were the first words that anyone had said in a while, and Katerina looked up at Cassiel with a start. He was staring at Dylan with a twinkle of mischief in his eyes, tired of his friend's passive-aggressive campaign. His long legs were stretched out on the ground beside the fire, and the corners of his lips twitched up as he stared across the flames.

Dylan glanced up in surprise as his hand drifted automatically to his face. "...What?"

Cassiel tilted back his head with a smile, the light of the fire dancing off his long white-blonde hair. "You look like you spent the day chewing on half the king's militia. That's all."

Oh, crap. Here we go.

Tanya spat out a mouthful of ale. Katerina paled, and glanced quickly across the flames. Sure enough, the left side of Dylan's face was still smeared with a generous helping of dried blood. She'd assumed he'd cleaned himself off around the same time he vanished into the woods to retrieve his clothes, but apparently he'd been a bit preoccupied and missed a spot. It was a testament to how fiercely he'd been ignoring her that she hadn't noticed it until now. And it was a testament to how utterly socially awkward Cassiel was that he'd dare to make a joke.

"It isn't entirely unflattering," the fae continued helpfully. "Quite the contrary. I think it brings out the seriousness in your eyes."

Cass—shut up!

At this point, Tanya was frozen between a gasp and a snicker. Katerina felt as though she was going to be sick. Dylan didn't say a word. He simply lifted his eyebrows as if to say *really*? But Cassiel played rough. His beautiful face shone with innocence as he gestured casually across the fire.

"I think you have a piece of bone in your hair."

THAT'S IT!

Katerina threw down her plate, about to give him a piece of her mind, but at the same time Dylan pushed abruptly to his feet. There wasn't a shred of emotion on his face as he put on his cloak and headed off into the trees.

"I'll take first watch," he called over his shoulder. "The rest of you should get some sleep."

He vanished into the shadows without another word, moving soundlessly over the soft blanket of leaves. It wasn't until he was nearly out of sight that he rubbed his face with his sleeve.

"Are you happy now?!" Katerina whipped back around to the fire with a furious hiss. "It wasn't enough that he had to kill those men, now you're giving him a hard time about it?!"

Much to her surprise, Cassiel wasn't at all fazed by the venom in her voice.

He simply leaned back against the rocks with a little smile, helping himself to what was left of Dylan's ale. "Dylan doesn't care about diminishing the royal army, Your Highness, and I wasn't giving him a hard time. I was giving him a new target for all that rage. And I was giving you an opening."

There was something unbearably sarcastic about the way he said 'Your Highness,' but there was something oddly sweet about it as well. As Katerina looked on in shock, he tilted his head gently towards the woods. The same place where Dylan had vanished just moments before.

"Go talk to him. Fix it."

She couldn't believe what she was hearing. Not socially awkward after all. Surprisingly...insightful.

"Well, would you look at that." Tanya seemed to be having the same revelation. "It seems there's more going on in that pretty head of yours than we gave you credit for."

Cassiel shot her a chilling look, but it melted quickly into a smile. "I just wanted his drink..."

A rush of gratitude welled up in Katerina's chest, but it would have to wait. Cassiel knew his friend well, and he was right. There had been a chip in the ice. A crack in the impenetrable wall of silence. If there was ever a time to mend fences, this was it.

She leapt to her feet the next moment, forgetting her cloak entirely as she went racing off into the trees. The dark night embraced her, removing every trace as she stumbled blindly across the forest floor. Past one embankment. Down another. The crescent moon provided little light to navigate, let alone search by, but she knew it wouldn't be a problem. This was *Dylan*.

She wouldn't have to find him. It would only be a matter of time before he found—

"Making a break for it?"

She heard him before she saw him. That quiet sigh, the same one he'd had as a wolf. Her feet froze on the forest floor, and a second later he walked out from between the trees. Bathed in a faint silver glow from the waning moon. His bright eyes resting gently on her face.

"Oh, you know..." Emboldened by Cassiel's success, she tried for some light-hearted banter of her own. Walking cautiously towards him all the while. "I thought I might go for a swim. See what mischief I can find..."

He sighed again but didn't turn away as she joined him by the edge of the trees. The anger that had defined him all day had gentled into something else. Something approachable. Something that gave her the courage to look him in the eyes.

"Dylan...I'm so sorry."

He looked down at her but said nothing. A virtual war of emotions was battling just behind his eyes. A dozen different feelings, each fighting for supremacy.

"It was stupid," she continued softly, bowing her head with shame. "You were right. It was stupid, and selfish, and I should have known better—"

"It wasn't stupid or selfish."

Her head snapped up, convinced she'd heard him wrong. "...Pardon?"

"It wasn't stupid or selfish," he repeated quietly, raking his fingers back through his hair with another quiet sigh. "You thought you saw a kid in trouble. You were trying to help. That isn't stupid or selfish. Exactly the opposite. And then, for your kindness...you were attacked."

His voice tightened at the last word, and the two of them lapsed into silence once more. For her part, Katerina had no idea what was going on. A part of her thought he might just be messing with her. Another part felt like maybe she should be making a break for it after all.

"Then," she lifted her eyes tentatively, trying her best to understand, "then why did you—"

"I couldn't track you. I couldn't find you." He repeated his exact words from before. If Katerina had to guess, she'd say he'd been repeating them in his head every minute since. A faint tremble shook his body, and without seeming to think about it he reached out and took her hand. "If I hadn't decided to head west... If I hadn't heard them talking..."

"I know," she said quietly.

"You can't do that to me." A trace of that same panic shone in his eyes. That frenzied fear from the clearing. "You can't put me in a position where I'm not able to..."

He trailed off. Uncharacteristically helpless, fighting things beyond his control.

"...where I'm not able to save you."

His fingers tightened around hers, and Katerina pulled in a sudden breath. All at once, she understood. His day of silent rage. His inability to look her in the eyes. Right down to him lashing out at her in the woods. It was misdirected rage. Cassiel had known it. Now she did, too. She was always a step behind.

Dylan wasn't blaming her. He was blaming himself.

They stood in silence for a while, each one lost to their thoughts, before she looked up with a tentative smile. "How did you find me now?"

He looked down in surprise, as if she'd called him back from somewhere very far away, then his lips curved up in a crooked grin. "I tracked you."

"You tracked me?" Katerina repeated in surprise. "But I thought—"

"Something changed. Broke your little spell."

She considered this for a long moment. On the one hand, she should be terrified that her last bit of magical protection from home had finally disappeared. On the other hand, she was almost pleased to see it go. It was quiet for a moment before she lifted her head, staring deep into his eyes. "Maybe I wanted to be found."

Then it came without warning—their first kiss.

One second, he was staring down at her in the darkness, frozen perfectly still. The next, he was lifting her into the air. His arms circling around her back as his lips closed over hers, sending little sparks of electricity and heat shooting over her skin.

She barely had time to register what was going on. She barely had time to catch her breath before she was overwhelmed completely. Her eyes closed of their own accord as her fingers knotted clumsily in his hair. Anything to keep him close. Anything to keep the kiss going.

A second later his tongue was in her mouth, and she let out a soft moan.

This can't be happening. I can't believe this is happening.

Her legs hitched around his waist, and the kiss deepened. His hands slid down her lower back. They grabbed fistfuls of her dress, aching to rip it off. She didn't know whether she wanted that to happen or not. She didn't know if she was ready for any of this to happen, or if it was just the adrenaline, and the night, and the magic of the moon.

"Dylan..."

She whispered his name before she could stop herself. Was it to stop him? Was it to encourage him? She didn't know. It was so quiet, there was a chance he wouldn't even hear.

But, of course, he did.

A rush of cold air sprang between them as he pulled away. A second later, her feet landed back on the ground. They burned and tingled as the blood returned to them, and no matter what she did she couldn't seem to catch her breath. Neither could he. They were both quietly panting.

There was a moment of awkward silence as the two of them stood there, looking anywhere except at each other, then he cocked his head suddenly towards the camp.

"You should get some sleep." His dark hair spilled into his eyes. Messy—where her fingers had knotted through. "We have a long day tomorrow."

Her eyes widened as she stared up at him in shock. Had she done something wrong? Was he angry? Upset? Feeling just as confused as she was feeling herself? "Dylan, I—"

A soft finger brushed against her lips. Silencing the words that would never come. "Get some sleep, princess."

He left without another word. Left her standing alone in the forest. Gazing helplessly after him in the dark. Her hands touching her mouth as the warmth of the kiss faded quickly from her lips.

Chapter 2

T hey say that people dream as a way of sorting out their feelings. That dreams are the mind's subconscious method of making sense of the world. Of coming to terms with things that have happened. Of coming to terms with things yet to come.

Katerina dreamt that she was back in the palace library, perched atop a mountain of books, trying to find a recipe for stew, while a giant duck quacked orders at her from the veranda.

Riddle me that.

When she opened her eyes what felt like a very short time later, the tent was empty. The men were already long gone, scouting ahead the day's journey. And judging by the smell of smoke and burnt meat, Tanya was obviously in the middle of some failed breakfast preparation.

The princess sat up slowly. Letting her eyes adjust to the morning light. Letting one hand drift slowly to her lips as she replayed it again and again. Wondering if it really happened.

There should really be a manual for these sorts of things. Midnight kisses in the woods. And for men! There should really be a manual for men!

She hardly even remembered getting back to the tent last night. Her mind had been so preoccupied with other things, it was a wonder she had made it to the campsite at all.

Had he been angry with her for stopping things? *Had* she stopped things, or had the whisper been one of encouragement, urging him quietly forward? If she didn't know herself, what could *he* possibly be thinking? And on that note—

HOLY HOUND DOGS! HE KISSED ME!

On that point, at least, she was perfectly clear. The rest of the night might be foggy, but the kiss itself she didn't think she'd ever be able to forget. The strength of his hands as he lifted her clear off the ground. The smell of his hair as it brushed against her face. The taste of his mouth as his tongue eased hers open, as forceful as he was gentle. As tender as he was strong.

"You never forget your first kiss."

It was something her governess had told her. Helene Vansprout. A woman with a face like an ox, but the heart of the mother the princess never had. Considering her charge was six years old at the time, she'd offered very little advice about men. But those words, Katerina never forgot.

"You never forget your first kiss."

The princess smiled to herself, her face warming with the light of the sun. No matter how confusing it had been. No matter how sudden, she knew she'd never want to. Then the smile faded to a worried frown. She could only speak for herself. The question was...did Dylan feel the same?

"Son of a harpy!"

Katerina's inner contemplation screeched to a halt as she gazed out the tent flap with a fond grin. Tanya may have pulled off a truly spectacular stew—one that had more to do with her entry into the gang than either Dylan or Katerina was prepared to admit—but those skills vanished completely when it came to breakfast. Chances were, the men had long since finished scouting and were simply keeping their distance until the smoke and the vile fumes had cleared.

Katerina pulled in a huge breath of air and coughed it back out. She didn't blame them.

"Kat, is that you?" Tanya's voice sounded as relieved as it was panicked. "You awake?"

It was one of Katerina's favorite things about the shifter. Her unwavering ability to go with the flow. Despite the royal revelation in the woods, Tanya carried on as if nothing extraordinary had happened. She was still Tanya. The princess was still Kat.

"Seriously, if you're awake, get your butt out here! This whole place is about to blow!"

Katerina stifled a giggle, and quickly shimmied into her clothes. It was a tight fit. With four bodies and four different packs crammed into one little tent, things were significantly more crowded than when it had just been her and Dylan.

Then again, last night might have gone very differently if it had just been her and Dylan.

"Katerina!"

Right. "I'm coming!"

She laced up the back of her dress, pulled on her boots, and shook out her fiery hair as she ducked under the flap and made her way into the clearing. Sure enough, the breakfast debacle was well under way. Aside from the noxious fumes, a thin layer of what looked like greenish fog had started streaming over the sides of the caldron hanging atop the fire. It crept over the ground like a hellish mist, contaminating everything in its path. Katerina could swear some of the flowers on the edge of the campsite had started to wilt.

"Smells good."

Tanya shot her an acidic look. She was perched upon a rock overlooking the caldron. A weapon in one hand, and a flask in the other. It was unclear as to which she needed more. "Laugh all you want. When Dylan and Cass get back, I'm telling them you did it."

Katerina grinned and fished around in her pack, pulling out a tin of biscuits and tossing one to the shifter. Tanya caught it on the edge of her knife and took a reluctant bite. When the caldron started emitting a low-pitched whine, she jumped down with a sigh and kicked dirt over the fire.

"Another one bites the dust."

Katerina sat down as far away from the mess as was polite, chewing thoughtfully on a biscuit of her own. "What's with the knife?"

Tanya's eyes drifted from the blade to the caldron, narrowing into a petulant sulk. "At one point, I thought there was a chance it had come to life..."

Wisely steering the conversation past the disastrous breakfast, Katerina patted the rock beside her and Tanya sat down. The two girls ate in silence for a while, casting occasional looks at the withering flames as the pot shuddered and creaked its death throes. Finally, after enough time had passed, Tanya cast the princess a sideways glance.

"So, what ended up happening last night?"

A piece of biscuit lodged in Katerina's throat, and she dissolved into a fit of frantic coughing. The flask was held out a moment later, and she took a giant gulp.

"Holy hound dogs!" She cursed and wiped her mouth with the back of her hand, behavior that would have gotten her skinned alive back at the palace. "How can you guys drink that stuff?"

Tanya shrugged and took another sip for herself. "After a while, you just go numb."

Not sure if that's a point in its favor...

The princess shuddered and smoothed down her dress, hyper aware that the shifter's eyes were still on her. When she made no effort to speak, Tanya tried again.

"So?"

"So, what?"

"Dylan!" Tanya laughed, forcing the flask back into Katerina's hand and indicating for her to take another sip. "What happened the other night with Dylan? Was he pretty ticked?"

The second sip went down a little easier than the first. The third was even easier after that.

"He *was* ticked," Katerina admitted, wiping her mouth again and passing back the flask. "But I don't think it was at me. At least if he was, he never said."

"You're lucky," Tanya muttered, downing the top half of the bottle. Katerina shot her a curious look and she rolled her eyes. "He was certainly ticked at me, let me tell you. If Cass hadn't finally intervened this morning, I think he'd still be yelling."

"Yelling?" Katerina turned to her in shock. "But for what?! You didn't do anything—"

"I let you out of my sight," Tanya interrupted quietly. "He was right to yell. I shouldn't have let the witches send you out by yourself. If I hadn't, none of this would have happened."

"That's ridiculous!" Katerina exclaimed, feeling an overwhelming surge of guilt. "I was the one who took off after the kid. It had nothing to do with you! It was completely *my* fault!"

"And that's what I told Dylan," Tanya said cheerfully. "Not that I blame you myself, but I needed to point the finger someplace else. That man can be intense."

Katerina took another look at her, then burst out laughing. She could go with the flow, all right. It seemed there was nothing in the world that wouldn't roll off the girl's back. "Well, thanks—for blaming me."

Tanya passed back the flask with a bright smile. "Cheers!"

They drank in silence for a while longer, completely ignoring the fact that it was early in the morning and they had a terribly long day ahead. Truth be told, Katerina was having trouble sorting through the events of the last twenty-four hours, and a stiff drink of whiskey could only help. That, and some gentle encouragement from her new, semi-demented friend.

"I didn't know he could shift."

Katerina almost dropped the flask right then and there. Oh, yeah. Not only had Dylan kissed her, but the man was a freakin' WOLF! She knew one or two details had slipped her mind...

She was quiet for a moment, then dropped her gaze to the ground. "Neither did I."

Tanya looked over in surprise. She had obviously been expecting the opposite. "You really didn't know? And he just burst into the clearing all wolfed out and started eating people?"

"He didn't eat them," Katerina began defensively. Then she thought back to the second guard and amended her answer. "He maybe just mauled them a little."

Tanya snorted with laughter, finding inexplicable humor in the words where the princess could not. "Well, everyone has their quirks, right? What did he say about it last night?"

Katerina's head snapped up, looking at her in surprise. "Excuse me?"

"Last night," Tanya said again, oblivious to her friend's reaction. "When you were talking to him last night, what did he say about the whole wolf thing?"

The hits just kept coming. Of all the things *not* to talk about. Of all the questions not to ask. The fact that he'd shifted into a giant wolf? *That* one had slipped her mind?

"It didn't..." She trailed off, the happy buzz from the whiskey faded, leaving her feeling suddenly cold. "It didn't come up."

Somewhere between him kissing me and him sending me away...it didn't come up.

"Whiskey for breakfast?"

The girls looked up with a start as the men marched back into the clearing. They'd obviously sensed the danger had passed, because when they saw the dirt-smothered fire neither looked surprised.

Cassiel nudged the edge of it with his boot before shooting Tanya a roguish wink. "A girl after my own heart."

"Run fast and far," Dylan teased, ruffling Tanya's hair as he walked past. She grinned back and tossed him the remainder of the flask. The two had obviously gotten past whatever trouble they'd had that morning.

Katerina could only hope she could say the same.

"Good morning," she ventured tentatively, hardly daring to glance up as Dylan slipped off his pack and tossed it beside the tent.

There was a split-second pause before he flashed her a quick smile. "Morning." Another incriminating pause. "How did you sleep?"

Katerina felt like she was choking on the biscuit again. Only this time, there was no biscuit. "...I dreamt I was making stew for a duck."

This time, the pause was much more pronounced. Dylan's eyebrows lifted slowly into his hair before his face lit with the makings of a genuine smile. "Me, too. What are the odds?"

Katerina snorted, and hopped down off the rock. "You're an exceptionally terrible liar, you know that?" She hesitated a moment, then added, "Especially for a shifter."

He'd been in the process of taking down the tent, but the second she said the word his hands froze above the rope. There was an almost imperceptible stiffening in his shoulders, and although he'd clearly heard what she'd said he didn't turn back around.

A second later, he continued with the rope.

"Oh yeah?" There was a note of caution to his voice, despite how hard he was trying to keep it light. "And how do you feel about that?"

Well, if he won't come to me, I'll just have to go to him.

Katerina dropped her pack and circled around to the back of the tent to help him. Her fingers wrapped around the loop of the rope he was unable to reach, and with a little tug the entire thing came free. His eyes flickered to hers as the canopy fell, just in time to see her flash a little grin. "I think I preferred the theory of the travelling circus thief."

THE NEXT FEW HOURS passed by in a sort of blur. Yes, the hike was brutal. Yes, the air was getting thinner and cooler the higher up they climbed. But, unlike the previous day, there was no layer of tension weighing them down. Things felt lighter. Conversation was funny and free. By the time they'd reached their designated stopping point for lunch, spirits were at an all-time high.

Of course, that's when the banter faded, and the bickering began.

"—which is why I warned you," Tanya was gesticulating wildly, trying to make the two much taller men standing on either side see reason, "I'm a heavy sleeper."

"Yes, you said you were a heavy sleeper," Cassiel retorted. "You didn't say that you were an inconvenient one. Never in my life would I imagine such a small girl could take up so much space."

Katerina stifled a grin as Dylan splintered away from them to join her. Last night might have been a blur, but she had vague recollections of what they were talking about. A vague memory of Tanya sprawling out in the tiny tent like some deranged starfish, either kicking or punching everyone who lay in her path. Cassiel, the poor man, had awoken with a black eye.

"It's not my fault!" she cried. "I'm used to having space. And I don't see why you should have more than me, just because you're about nine feet tall!"

The fae glared down at her like he was just inches away from showing her what that powerful frame of his could do. To make things even, Tanya shifted into him on the spot.

"Don't do that!" Cassiel shouted, leaping back in alarm while gawking at his life-size reflection. "I thought we took a vote and agreed you can't do that!"

"Do what?" Tanya asked, in a voice much deeper than her own. Cassiel's lovely features twisted into Tanya's signature smirk. "I'm just evening the playing field."

Katerina and Dylan started snickering as one Cassiel began mimicking the other's furious gestures. It wasn't long before said gestures turned violent, and one grabbed the other by the throat.

"Dylan, make her shift back!"

"I can't breathe, you lunatic! Let me go!"

"What do you think?" Katerina stretched up onto her tiptoes, whispering into the ranger's ear. "Should we give them a few minutes, or pull them apart?"

Dylan grinned, watching as the two of them struggled. "Oh, I think we can give it a few minutes. This is way too much fun."

"For bloody sake, woman!" Cassiel gritted his teeth, catching 'himself' in a headlock and kicking out his own legs with one swift blow. "Do you have any idea what kind of therapy I'm going to need to get past this?!"

"It's your own flippin' fault! No one likes a sore loser!" Tanya fell to the ground, reaching up at the same time to feel her new pointed ears. "...this is weird."

Katerina laughed along with Dylan, until something fluttering along the edge of the little clearing caught her eye. Curious, she left the others behind, walking slowly across the tall grass.

It was a paper, she realized. A flyer that had been nailed into the tree.

A faint frown flitted across her face as she instinctively glanced around. They were tens of miles away from the nearest settlement. They had put actual mountains between themselves and the nearest road. But the flyer looked brand new. Where could it have come from?

"Kat?"

She glanced behind her, to see Dylan jogging swiftly across the field. Behind him, one Cassiel was slowly choking the other to death. A look of concern flashed across his face as he examined her. He had not yet seen the poster.

"What happened? What's wrong?"

She didn't say anything. She merely pointed to the tree.

His eyes found it at once, latching on as a similar look of wonder flashed across his face. A guarded wariness was soon to follow, and it was with great caution that he approached the tree. The princess hung back as he ripped the paper from off the tree, taking a second to read it.

This can't be good.

Every ounce of color drained from his face, leaving a pale statue standing there. He opened his mouth once to speak, then closed it. He opened it again but thought better of it each time. Instead, he pulled in a deep breath, crumpled up the paper, and stuffed it deep inside his pocket.

In a flash, Katerina sprang back to life.

"What is it? What did it say?"

By now, the others were behind her. Tanya had returned to her normal form, looking a little worse for wear, and she and Cassiel were standing side by side with matching looks of worry.

Dylan glanced at them once before shaking his head with an almost believable air of nonchalance. "Nothing. It was old. About some festival that's already done."

Not one of them was fooled. Not one.

"That's funny," Katerina took a step forward, folding her arms across her chest with an accusatory glare, "I thought we just established that you're a *terrible* liar. What does it say, Dylan? Tell me!"

He hesitated briefly, shared a quick glance with Cassiel, then seemed to realize it was inevitable. With a soft sigh, he pulled the paper out of his pocket and tossed it her way. She caught it with trembling hands. Hands that went dead still when she unfolded it and saw what it had to say.

The first thing that caught her attention was the royal seal. The next thing was the headline.

Katerina Damaris
Accused of High Treason for the Murder of the King

Reward for Immediate Capture

She read the words in a daze, staring blankly at her picture below. The paper had all but fallen from her hands before she saw the last words. Soon to be burned forever into her mind.

Dead or Alive

Chapter 3

The paper slipped noiselessly from Katerina's hands, but she felt as if there should have been a deafening *boom* as it landed inaudibly on the tall grass. There had been a silent aftershock as her friends absorbed the information, but already a frantic, murmured conversation was getting underway. Not that she really heard it. She couldn't hear anything past the dull ringing in her ears.

Kailas is blaming me. He's saying I did it.

It shouldn't have come as a huge surprise. In hindsight, she probably should have seen it coming. If her brother would go so far as to murder their father then, surely, he wouldn't hesitate to shift the blame. But no matter how logical it all sounded, the princess found herself completely unable to come to terms. In a bizarre way, it was almost harder to believe that he would publicly blame her than it was to comprehend the murder itself. Her own brother. Her own brother did this.

He's blaming me. He's saying I did it.

"—doesn't change a thing."

"Like hell it doesn't! It changes everything!"

"Just calm down for a second, and let me—"

"No, I'm not going to calm down," Tanya hissed. Her hazel eyes flickered around the little clearing, as if the world had shrunk dramatically since the last time she looked. "They put it up *here*, Dylan. You found it right *here* on this tree. In the heart of the Black Forest. An entire mountain range away from the nearest signs of life. They were *here*."

"The girl is right." Cassiel might look the same age as the rest of them, but in times of trouble it was suddenly easy to remember he'd been alive for almost a century. "This changes things. We're going to have to double our pace. Make for the safe house with all speed."

Tanya had been nodding along but stopped abruptly when he got to the end.

"What—no! That's not what I'm saying at all!" She may have been about half his size, but she more than made up for it with intensity. "We need to forget about Brookfield and find someplace closer to hide. We stay out in the open, we're dead."

He's blaming me. He's saying I did it.

"Why do you think we're going to Brookfield?" Cassiel countered sharply. "There isn't a better place in this world *to* hide."

"Yes, but it's at least another week's journey. Maybe more." Tanya shook her head quickly, her cinnamon hair swishing against the tops of her shoulders. "At least one troop of guards was up here to post that banner. Maybe more. We're not going to last another week."

Dylan looked between them. Unwilling to commit either way.

"None of us is safe. Anywhere. Brookfield is our best option." Cassiel crossed his arms over his chest.

It was a good sign that neither one of them had talked about jumping ship. After all, the banner mentioned only the princess, none of her accomplices. But they were both making valid arguments, and at the moment Dylan looked unsure which way to decide. His eyes flickered once or twice to Katerina, but she was still lost in her own world.

High treason. He's saying I killed Father.

"—not a matter of experience," Tanya was shouting. "This is basic common sense!"

"It's a knee-jerk reaction," Cassiel replied with increasingly strained patience. "One based in panic instead of clear thought. We are going where they cannot follow. That's the entire point—"

"Kailas said I did it."

The heated argument came to a sudden halt as all three of them turned around slowly to look at the princess. She was standing exactly where she'd been when she'd read the poster. She hadn't blinked, breathed, or moved an inch. A strange ashen tinge was spreading its way over her fair skin, as if she had blown into a cloud of chalk, and despite the sun having come out and it being very warm she was trembling.

"He said I killed my father."

The words were disjointed and clipped. Looping endlessly through her mind. Like the worst sort of dream—one from which she was unable to wake.

The others shared a nervous glance while Dylan stepped cautiously forward. Moving with exaggerated slowness, as if at any moment she might bolt and run away.

"Yes, he did," he said quietly. "Kailas said that." Another step closer, his eyes never left her face. "But Kat, this isn't—"

But whatever he was going to say, she didn't hear him. The next second, she was gone.

"KAT!"

The two of them tore through the trees. One chasing after another. The world flew past in a beautiful sea of green, but neither one noticed. They were looking straight ahead.

"Kat, slow down!"

It was ridiculous that a ranger would make such a request. But between the whiskey, the wanted poster, and her blind adrenaline, she was storming straight through things he was taking care to avoid. Brambles. Boulders. Frigid mountain streams. By the time he finally caught up with her, she looked as though she'd been dropped from a cliff in the middle of a temperate rain storm.

"*Katerina.*"

He caught her by the wrist, easing her to a gentle stop. Just as gently, he turned her towards him. Taking only a moment to examine her wide, vacant eyes, before pulling her into his chest.

"I'm sorry," he breathed, bringing up one hand to stroke the back of her hair. "Your own brother, I can't even...I'm so sorry, Kat."

She stood there and let herself be held. Only half-registering the contact. The other half was still frozen back in the clearing. Staring down at those three fateful words.

Dead or Alive

"He killed my ladies, you know?"

Dylan stiffened, then looked down at her in surprise. She hadn't said the words with any particular inflection, but they were shocking nonetheless.

"...I didn't know."

Of course, he didn't. No one did. But she was too far gone to realize that now.

"I sent them away from me," she continued in that hollow, vacant voice. "Ordered them to stay in the palace. Protect their families and submit to the new rule."

A faint shudder rippled through her body. He absorbed it into his hands.

"When I went back to get my necklace, they were lying on the floor. Dead. Stacked in some huge, bloody pile, like someone was trying to save space. Dead."

Again, he stiffened. This time, he had no idea what to say.

The people scattered around the outer rim of the kingdom had all grown up with stories of the crown prince. They knew well of his cruelty, his greed. While the princess might have known a rosier version of him up until recently, the others had long since been disillusioned.

This poster clearly did not surprise him. But saying that wouldn't help.

"I don't understand why he had to do that," Katerina said faintly. Her face was still pressed up against Dylan's chest, but the quiet words came through loud and clear. "It wasn't like I was taking them with me. I was alone. He...he knew them. We grew up together. Why would he—"

"For exactly that reason," Dylan interrupted gently. "To isolate you. To cut you off from everyone you know and make you feel entirely alone."

It was quiet for a moment, then he tilted up her head.

"...but you're not."

She gazed up at him, her eyes shining with a hundred tears.

"You're not alone," he said again, quiet but firm. "You have people who are willing to fight for you. People who are willing to risk everything. You have me—" He cut off suddenly, editing on the fly. "I mean...you have us. Me and Tanya and Cass. We're not going anywhere. I promise."

For a moment, their eyes locked. He wiped away a stray tear that had fallen and she managed to take her first deep breath. Then, just as quickly as they'd come together, she pulled away.

"Just three more people who are going to die because of me." She took a step back, her worn boots landing softly upon the damp leaves. "And as for us?" Their eyes locked again, before she turned away. "There is no us. You made that perfectly clear."

BY THE TIME THEY GOT back to their little camp, the others had come to some sort of tentative truce. For at least the time being, they'd decided to go with Cassiel's plan. They would continue to Brookfield as they'd been doing. Only with one or two minor adjustments to the route.

"What about Clever's Pass?" Tanya was saying. "Even in the summer, it's almost always deserted. If we're really trying to stay under the radar, that would be our best bet."

Cassiel frowned to himself, deep in thought. "It's a hard climb. Even under the best of circumstances. And the weather has been unseasonably cold. I'm not sure if—"

"We're not going to Clever's Pass," Katerina said quietly. The others looked up in surprise, their eyes flashing from her to Dylan then back to her. "We're not going anywhere. Not together."

They absorbed this for a moment.

Then Tanya shook her head. "Kat, if you're talking about splitting up, that's a *really* stupid idea—"

"We're not splitting up," Katerina replied firmly. "We're parting ways. I appreciate what you've all done for me, what you've been willing to risk—but I'm not. Willing to risk it, that is. I'm not willing to risk any of you."

Cassiel lifted his eyebrows in surprise, while Dylan turned away to the trees. Tanya, on the other hand, was outraged. And it was an emotion she seldom kept to herself.

"Well, fortunately, *Your Highness*, it's not up to you. Right?" She looked around at the others for support. "We decided to embark upon this together. As a group. You can't just—"

"I can, and I just did." Katerina picked up her pack and swung it over her shoulders. "I won't have any more blood on my hands. Especially that of the three of you. I simply can't permit it."

For the first time, Cassiel was looking at her with a hint of respect, but Tanya absolutely wasn't having it. "Well, that's total bull—"

"Where will you go?" Dylan interrupted quietly.

Katerina turned towards him, but before she could say a word Tanya leapt in between.

"Are you serious?" she hissed. "Dylan, you can't possibly—"

"Where will you go?" he said again, eyes locked solely on the princess.

Katerina considered the question for the first time. Things were changing so quickly, she honestly hadn't given it much thought. Not that she knew much about the mountain terrain anyway.

After a long moment, she simply gestured up the nearest hill.

"That way."

Cassiel followed the gesture with a frown, Tanya cursed under the breath, but Dylan never broke her gaze. A faint look of amusement danced across his face, but he didn't smile. He simply picked up his pack and slipped it over his shoulders.

"How strange." He tilted his head towards the same hill. "As fate would have it, we're heading 'that way' too."

WHAT HAPPENED BACK in the clearing with the poster was supposed to have been a personal revelation. An impassioned stand after which Katerina struck out on her own forever. Exposed and defenseless against the dangers of the world, but with a clear conscience and unwavering beliefs.

It was not supposed to turn into a woodland game of hide and seek.

In the beginning, Katerina had thought they would just lose interest. That if she simply ignored them and continued on her own, they would eventually realize she was serious, give up the ghost, and head back to their respective homes.

She'd done all she could to see it through.

She'd set out immediately without giving them time to pack up their things. She'd embarked upon a nonsensical course, darting through the trees in illogical zig-zags that left her feeling dizzy but satisfied she could not be followed. She'd even doubled back once or twice before abruptly changing direction. At the last moment, she headed for the mountains instead.

Why wasn't she surprised, then, when she heard three familiar voices ringing in the trees?

"I say good riddance," Tanya was saying loudly, pushing noisily through the branches, completely oblivious to the fact that she was snapping them back in Cassiel's face. "Sure, she might come off as sweet in the beginning, but the girl is a royal pain in the ass. *Plus*, she ruined breakfast."

Katerina snorted in laughter, then forced that smile into a scowl as she quickened her clumsy pace. Only a few seconds later, she heard the others. They weren't behind her, as she'd originally thought, but were walking side by side. Just about fifty yards to her right.

"I caught her rummaging through my pockets in the middle of the night," Cassiel added seriously. "Probably looking for money, the little thief."

For a second Katerina almost lost her composure entirely, ready to launch all her defenses. Then she glanced out of the corner of her eye, took one look at the innocent face, and remembered to hold her tongue. They weren't going to get her so easily.

Dylan had no stories to contribute. No slurs against her character, no baiting or lies. He kept mostly to himself and let the others do the talking. Opening his mouth only occasionally to remind them to slow their pace: "Apparently, we are to climb this mountain at the speed of a drunken child."

Katerina bit her lip to conceal a smile. She figured that last bit was for her.

And, so, it continued. When she hiked, they hiked. When she rested, they rested. When she got lost and took an hour-long detour to avoid a river they rolled their eyes, complained, but did the same.

Things remained fairly consistent until the four of them set up camp for the night. Two separate camps. Just a stone's throw away. But only one of them had a tent. And food. And a fire.

Katerina brought her arms up around her chest and shivered violently as she watched them jealously through the trees. How it was they'd gotten a fire going out of the wet wood, she had no idea. She'd been trying for the last forty minutes with no success, but Cassiel had basically just touched the thing and it had sprung to life. She'd finally given up and was leaning against the trunk of a tall tree. Clutching her cloak around her. Nothing but a single biscuit to her name.

Just give it another night. They'll give up after another night and go home. Then you won't have to worry about them. Then they'll be safe.

The thought comforted her and terrified her all at the same time. Yes, she wanted them to be safe, but she couldn't imagine what it would be like when they were actually gone. Her mind flashed back to how she'd felt that first night, running away from the palace, completely alone in the trees, and she stifled a shudder. She may be freezing, and starving, and dying of thirst, but she was taking a considerable amount of comfort just in the sight of their tent. To have it all taken away?

It's what YOU wanted. It's what YOU insisted upon. Get on board.

With the world's quietest sigh, she curled up in a little ball on the ground and forced herself to close her eyes. If she could make it through the chilly night to morning without losing any of her toes, she'd count it as a success. And if she had one more night's security, knowing that people who cared about her were close by...she might as well enjoy it while she could.

And so, with the sounds of a distant fire crackling in her ears, she drifted off into the world's most troubled sleep. At least, that's what she tried to do.

Three hours later, she was still awake.

The fire next door had long since died, and there were no sounds coming from the tent. The others were no doubt fast asleep, but the icy mountain chill was making that virtually impossible. She sucked a freezing breath through her teeth and huddled down as far as she could in her cloak. It was fine while she was up and moving about but wasn't designed to act as a blanket. Even now, it had accumulated so much water that she was thinking of casting it off entirely.

A sudden noise in the trees made her sit up with a start. Her eyes widened with fear as she looked around, while her trembling fingers groped around blindly for a rock or a stick. Anything she could use as a weapon. The higher up they'd climbed into the mountains, the more tracks they'd stumbled across from nature's finest predators. Wolves, cougars, and bears. She wouldn't be at all surprised if one had happened upon her in the night, prowling about for an easy snack.

"Hello?" she whispered, hardly daring to speak.

There was another noise. Much closer than the first. She carefully lifted the rock above her head, then froze perfectly still. Too frightened to move. A final twig snapped, and she almost fainted right then and there.

"No need for the rock. I surrender."

It fell from her hands as her body wilted with an exhausted sigh. A second later, Dylan stepped through the trees. He was carrying a flagon of water and a heavy blanket.

"I thought you were a bear," she confessed weakly, bringing her knees up to her chest.

His eyes made a quick study before twinkling with his signature smile. "Not a bear. A wolf, remember?"

She was too cold to even laugh at the joke, and he settled down beside her. A second later, he'd spread the blanket across the two of them and pressed the water into her hand. When she looked up at him, he ignored her with a dismissive shrug.

"I'm cold."

Her icy lips twitched up into a smile. *Right. I bet you are.*

A second after that, he leaned back against the tree. Unlike her, who'd had to fidget and adjust for a small eternity before she could get comfortable, he looked as natural as could be. His eyes were closed, and one arm was slightly extended. A silent invitation for her to come inside.

An hour earlier, she might have refused. Now, bordering on the fringes of frostbite, she no longer had that kind of pride.

Without a word, she shifted closer and nestled down into his arms. He smelled of leather and pine, and with a contented sigh she lay her head upon his chest and closed her eyes. Both arms wrapped instantly around her, and the heat from his skin seeped into her own. The sound of his steady heartbeat was like a drug, lulling her into a hypnotic sleep, but before she closed her eyes for good she tilted her head and asked him one final thing. "Why are you always saving me?"

His arms tightened as he glanced down with a smile. "Bad habit."

She absorbed this for a moment, blinking against the heavy fatigue. Then she lifted her chin again, peering up at him under the light of the moon. "The other night…why did you tell me to go to bed?"

It wasn't his fault that she could feel the sudden hitch in his breathing. That she felt the way his pulse hammered and his heart skipped a beat. It was quiet for a moment, before he gave an even quieter reply.

"I told you to go to bed because the day was over. I told you to go to bed because we had a long day ahead of us."

His tone ended the conversation, and she put the rest of her questions away for the time being. Her head dropped back against his chest, and before she knew it she was drifting off into a dreamless sleep.

She almost didn't hear him say the last part. She was almost too far gone.

"I told you to go to bed." The wind swept down upon them, and his arms tightened around her again. "I didn't say I didn't want to go with you."

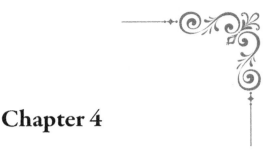

Chapter 4

Katerina opened her eyes the next morning, shocked to discover she was warm. The sun was out, and she was still cradled snugly against Dylan's chest. Her body rose and fell with his steady breathing, and every now and then one of his fingers would twitch in a dream.

A secret smile curled up the side of her face, and she cuddled in closer. Over the last several weeks the two of them had spent many nights together, but there had never been anything like this.

Especially after that kiss. Especially after what he said last night.

The smile grew brighter as she watched his fingers, fighting imaginary demons and monsters in his sleep. Despite the rough exterior and the 'Get lost' attitude, there were times he reminded her of a child. Brimming with energy. Searching for adventure. Sparkling eyes fixed on the horizon.

He probably thinks I didn't hear. He probably thought I was asleep already.

But the words were burned forever into her mind. They'd electrified her body and kept her awake long after he'd passed out himself. *"I told you to go to bed...I didn't say I didn't want to go with you."* After getting over the initial shock, the initial flattery, the initial cheek-blazing blush that immediately followed, Katerina did her best to consider the possibility from all sides.

Was that something she wanted? Did she even care about him like that? When two people were joined at the hip, living each day on the edge of a knife, it was hard to tell one way or another.

What feelings were real? How deep did they run? Did Dylan feel any of them, too?

The smile faded a little as she considered this.

It had only taken a few days on the road for her to realize that the man eclipsed her in terms of experience. A dozen pairs of lusty eyes followed wherever he went, a dozen lusty stories were attached to every town, and it wasn't like he exactly shied away from the attention. He did when he was with her, of course, but the man obviously had game. And obviously enjoyed the company of women.

A night spent in her bed might be nothing more than casual for him. A way to pass the time and keep warm on the cold forest nights. No feelings involved whatsoever.

But it can't just be that, can it? Otherwise, why would he have sent me away? Why would he have stopped our kiss? Another thought occurred to her, and she froze. *Why the heck am I even thinking about all this, when my homicidal brother just put a price on my head?!*

He shifted suddenly beneath her, tightening his arms like she was some teddy bear, before his eyes fluttered open and shut. They focused slowly on the brilliant sunrise, drifting down to the girl in his arms. She was staring back up at him with a little smile.

"Good morning."

His lips twitched up, and he made no move to release her. "Morning. You still have all your toes?"

She rolled her eyes but wriggled them just to be sure. "Ten fingers, ten toes. All in all, I'd rate the night as a huge success."

He chuckled quietly and stretched out his long legs. She might be hyper-aware of the fact that their bodies were pressed up against each other, but he didn't seem to notice. One hand stayed pressed against her lower back as the other rummaged around and produced the flagon of water.

"You should drink something." It wasn't a suggestion, but a good-natured command. "You didn't have enough yesterday, and the last thing you want up here is to get dehydrated."

She unscrewed the cap carefully, peeking up occasionally through her lashes. "How do you know how much water I drank yesterday?"

"...lucky guess."

A little grin broke through, in spite of her best efforts, and she 'accidentally' spilled some on his stomach as she was screwing back on the cap. He tensed immediately, then scowled, then grinned, then sprayed her face with a handful of droplets.

Rangers can also be playful. Good to know.

They lay there for a while longer, passing the water back and forth, each secretly unwilling to let the other go, before the sounds from the camp next door started filtering through the trees. They glanced over at the same time, staring blankly through the tall redwoods, then dropped their heads with an identical sigh. Their brief respite was over. Time to get back to the real world.

"So, what's it going to be, princess?" Dylan asked as they finally untangled themselves, sitting up together and gazing out over the magnificent vista beyond. "Have you come to your senses, or are we going to keep playing follow-the-leader all over these hills?"

Katerina's eyes flickered over to the tent. Then to the breakfast fire crackling merrily in front of it. Then to the people gathered around that fire. She stared at them for a moment, taking in every single detail, and then the strangest thing happened. Along with the nauseating fear, and the worry, and the sense of doom that had been plaguing her since the moment she saw that poster, she began to feel the stirrings of something else, too. Something that felt a bit like hope.

"I think we'd better stick together," she said casually. "You three obviously need me. It's a miracle you lasted even the night."

Dylan nodded with a thoughtful frown, acting like it didn't bother him either way. The two of them quickly folded up the blanket and started heading back to the others. They'd almost made it all the way, when she heard him mutter under his breath. "Heaven forbid we pick a single direction and stick with it for the rest of the day..."

She smacked him as hard as she could, right in the center of the back.

"You just couldn't leave it alone, could you?" she demanded. "You just couldn't let this be one of those happy moments, and leave it at that?"

He kept walking with a little smile. "Heaven forbid we learn how to start a fire..."

THE OTHERS HANDLED Katerina's return to the fold with a lot more grace. Tanya caught her in a suffocating bear hug, then demanded she sample whatever was smoking above the flames. Even Cassiel, with whom she hadn't really bonded, gave her a one-armed hug before returning to his seat on the other side of the fire. She stared after him in surprise, wondering if she was ever going to figure out what was going on inside that capricious head of his.

They had been in the middle of an intense discussion before she arrived. Still deliberating as to the wisest route to Brookfield Hall. Apparently, none of them thought her little rebellion would last very long, and they wanted to be prepared the moment she came back.

"I still say that Clever's Pass is the best way to go." Tanya shielded her eyes and squinted with great authority towards the mountains in the distance. "I know it's not the easiest climb in the world, but I think we've proven ourselves by now, haven't we?"

Dylan's eyes flickered from the smoking caldron to the half-capsized tent, but he pursed his lips and said nothing. Instead, he turned to Cassiel. His reluctant voice of reason.

"It's a double-edged sword," the fae said thoughtfully. "It's a dangerous path, but that might mean it's the safest for people in our position to travel. The prince must have figured out by now that there are people out there working to keep the princess alive. He can't imagine we would risk her life by taking her somewhere like that."

Katerina shivered discreetly at the words 'somewhere like that.' If it was as dangerous as they were making it out to be shouldn't they, too, be avoiding it at all costs?

"What do you think?" she asked Dylan quietly. The others could input all they wanted, but she wouldn't go along with a plan until she heard it from his own mouth.

He considered the question for a long time, glancing up occasionally at the snowy peaks in the distance. When he finally answered, it was clear he was searching for the lesser of two evils.

"It's cold," he murmured, sticking his hands in his pockets as the icy wind swept his hair off his face. "It shouldn't be so cold this time of year."

Cassiel nodded slowly. Troubled by the same thing.

"Still, I think we should try it." His hand closed around the poster; he'd taken it with him before running off after Katerina in the woods. "I wouldn't have thought we'd still be seeing guards so far north, but here they are. Clever's Pass might be the only chance we have to lose them."

"So, it's decided." Tanya picked up her pack with a cheerful smile, unwilling to let even the worst of circumstances get her down. "Off to a frozen wasteland of death."

There was a heavy pause.

"Yeah...something like that."

The others gave her a long look, slowly following suit. They packed up the rest of the camp, scarfed down a quick bite of breakfast, and stamped out what remained of the fire.

Less than ten minutes later they were all standing in a line, staring out at the frozen mountains beyond.

They lingered there a moment, trying to make peace with the thought, before Dylan cocked his head and they started marching straight towards the summit.

He went out in front, his sharp eyes missing not a single detail as they made their way over the rugged terrain. Katerina followed just after, a great deal more scared than she was letting on but determined to keep pace. Cassiel was just a step behind. Tall and graceful. And wary. Keeping his eyes on the trees, as if at any moment a new danger might come leaping out. Tanya brought up the rear, humming quietly under her breath and pausing now and then to pick a stray flower.

They were an unusual group, but a determined one. The whimsical music and daisy chains certainly didn't help. The fae tolerated them for as long as he could before glaring over his shoulder.

"You were living as a goblin too long..."

IT DIDN'T TAKE LONG to get to the mountains. Another day hiking through the tall grass, and another night camping amongst the heather, and they were already there. What *did* take long, was getting through the mountains. After just a few hours of struggling through the snow, in clothes not at all suited, Katerina was beginning to doubt they'd ever make it to the other side.

"This...was maybe a bad idea."

A thick blanket of snow covered the ground, hiding dips and ravines and making everything look deceptively level. Every few minutes or so, one of them would sink into a waist-deep drift and need to be fished out by the others. Every few minutes or so, they would need to stop and shake a heavy coating of powder from their clothes. Fingers stiffened and cracked. Momentum stalled and grew sluggish. And conversations were soon reduced to the quickest grunt or shake of the head as they tried to conserve their energy for what was yet to come.

It was bad enough for Katerina, who had next to no experience and whose skinny body offered little protection from the cold. But poor Tanya had it even worse. The girl was scarcely taller than the goblin she'd been impersonating. Just a little over five feet. While the snow came up to the rest of their chests, it was coming up to her chin.

"I'm serious." The tiny girl pulled out a blade and started hacking furiously at the ice bank in front of her, trying to clear a path. "Next time I have a 'great idea,' punch me in the mouth."

"Duly noted."

She glanced up with a scowl as Cassiel swept past her. But while he might have been teasing, he was not unkind. Before she could take another step, he reached down and lifted her clear out of the snow, setting her on a firmer bit of ice on the other side of the embankment.

"Pointy-eared little troll..." Tanya muttered.

"You're welcome." Cass nodded once.

Katerina tried to smile, but her lips had hardened into a pale, thin line. Every breath was agony, and every step felt as though it might be the last one. Back in the forest, they'd climbed over two or three mountains every day. It was a grueling pace, but at least it was possible. But this?

The sun was starting to slip lower in the sky, and they hadn't even reached the first alpine peak. At this rate, there was little chance of them making it before nightfall. And even then, where in the world were they supposed to pitch the tent?

"Thinking warm thoughts?"

She glanced to the side and saw Dylan wading towards her through the snow. The tops of his cheeks were flushed with exertion, but the rest of him was pale white. The rest of him that she could see, at least. He'd covered his head in a scarf so that only a thin band revealing his eyes was visible. The brows above them had been coated white, making him look like a wizard in training.

"Does that ever work for you?" she panted back. "Thinking warm thoughts?" In her mind, it seemed almost spiteful. Why taunt herself when it felt like she would never be warm again?

She couldn't see much of his face, but she could have sworn he smiled.

"Don't tell me that you lose your sense of humor in the cold. I never would have suggested this place if I'd known. I would have insisted we travel by way of the beach."

She started to laugh, but miscalculated a step, and went tumbling head first straight into a high snow bank. Her arms flew up as she prepared to get a bloody mouthful of ice but a hand shot out at the last second, grabbing the back of her cloak and pulling her to firmer ground.

"No need to be so dramatic, princess." His eyes twinkled as he brushed a layer of frozen sleet off her back. "I'm already paying attention to you."

She wanted to punch him, but it would take too much energy. She wanted to scramble up onto his back and get out of the snow, but it struck her that might not be entirely fair. Instead, she gestured to Tanya, turning the spotlight away from herself.

"Why doesn't she just shift into someone taller?" she asked curiously. "Or into something with wings—avoid the climb altogether."

Dylan followed her gaze, watching the tiny girl struggle with an almost brotherly concern, before forcing it quickly from his eyes. "It takes an absurd amount of energy to shift into another sentient being. I'm guessing she doesn't have that kind of energy right now. And as for something that flies..." He trailed off, considering it for the first time. "I've heard rumors of that happening. Of people shifting into giant birds, or people with wings. But it's almost impossible. Especially for someone of Tanya's age. Give her fifty years or so...*maybe*. But not now. Certainly not in this place."

"No problem," Katerina panted. "I'm sure we'll still be here in fifty years." Dylan shot her a sideways grin as she tripped once more. "On that note, why *did* you suggest this place?"

His smile faded as he glanced warily up at the sky. "I'm beginning to wonder that myself."

As if on cue the clouds suddenly darkened, and a thick layer of snow began to fall. There was a series of muffled shouts and exclamations before the four of them clambered under the jagged edge of a snow-covered boulder and huddled together, staring miserably at the stormy skies.

"This shouldn't be happening," Cassiel said softly. It wasn't a complaint, it was merely a contemplation. One that sent chills running down Katerina's spine. "Not here. Not in the summer."

Dylan's face tightened, but he nodded. He'd clearly been thinking the same thing all day. "I know."

The sky above them screamed and roared. Daring them to keep talking about what should and shouldn't be. It looked as though the entire world was ripping apart. One seam at a time.

"In almost five hundred years, it's never—"

"I know."

The wind picked up speed, and the four of them huddled closer together. Without seeming to realize it, they all had a hand on each other. A fistful of jacket. The side of a sleeve. As the world around them fell apart, it seemed the only way to keep themselves together.

"Should we go back?" Tanya asked quietly. Her entire body was shaking, but she gazed at the storm with steady eyes. "Head out the way we came in? Wait for the storm to pass?"

Dylan nodded slowly, and Katerina sighed in relief. At this point, what was the alternative?

"We could certainly try." Cassiel's bright eyes squinted hard against the wind, gazing out in the opposite direction. "Take the lower trail. The one that dips down by the—"

It might have been a good idea. It might have been their very salvation. But they would never know. At that very moment, the clouds
ripped open with a flash of blinding light.

WHAT THE—?!

The princess let out a piercing scream as a giant bolt of lightning
sliced through the center of the sky, striking a mountain cliff behind
them. A curved, dome-like peak they'd passed under less than an hour
before. There was a deafening crash followed by an ominous rumble,
and then, for a split-second, the entire world seemed to stand still.

The four friends stared up in terror. Not daring to move. Not daring to breathe.

Please let it be okay. Please let it be okay.

Katerina took a step closer to Dylan as everything around them
went silent. The dizzying flurries. The thundering clouds. Even the
storm itself seemed to be waiting for something.

For a suspended moment, nothing happened. Then the entire
mountain began to give way.

Giant slabs of solid ice broke off the top. Thousands of tons of sleet
and snow fell in a morbidly beautiful cascade towards the earth. They
hit the ground with a noise that shattered Katerina's eardrums and rat-
tled her teeth. Then the four of them watched, in what felt like slow
motion, as the entire mountain of furious, icy death came flying their
way.

This is it. This is how we'll die.

The princess pulled in her breath for another scream, but there
wasn't time. Before she could inhale, a strong hand caught her by the
waist and shoved her down against the boulder. Her teeth sank into her
tongue and a burst of blood pooled in her mouth. She only barely had
time to roll onto her back before Dylan came down on top of her.

His eyes were frantic, and his skin was pale white. The scarf he'd
been using to protect himself flew off in the wind as he lowered his face
to hers, speaking directly into her ear.

"Just take a breath. I've got you."

How could he be so calm? In just seconds, the entire canyon would be covered in a suffocating layer of snow, and the four friends would be buried right along with it.

Out of the corner of her eye, she saw Cassiel pull Tanya down beside them. The two of them were crouched in the far corner beneath the dome of rock, holding onto each other for dear life in the precious few seconds that remained. Katerina looked at each one in turn, her ears ringing with the screaming wind, before turning back to Dylan.

Their eyes met, and for the second time in just a few seconds the world stood still.

She didn't think she'd ever be able to describe what passed between them in that frozen moment. There were worlds lost, dreams ended, and lives that would never be shared. But at the same time there was a strange sort of peace. A feeling of tranquility that spread through her, making her entire body go still.

With a shaking hand, she reached up and brushed a frozen lock of hair away from his eyes; the rest was dancing wildly in the wind. Her fingers lingered on his face, and when their eyes locked again the princess and the ranger shared the world's most unlikely of smiles.

Then the ice struck, and the entire world went dark.

There was no more smiling after that.

Chapter 5

It started as a dull ringing in her ears. That's the first clue Katerina had that told her she wasn't dead, but that some small part of her was still clinging to life. The ringing got louder and louder as she lay, perfectly suspended, in the snow.

It seems unfair, she thought, encased in her icy coffin, *that I would survive the initial blow, only to wake then have to suffocate. Why couldn't I have just died instantly? I bet the others got to.*

Not that she needed to breathe. Not that she felt particularly cold. It was like her body had gone into stasis, a frosty hibernation. She felt neither hurried, nor impatient. Neither worried, nor alarmed. She was simply there. But as the ringing in her ears intensified, she was beginning to realize she wasn't the only one...

Ringing became vibration. Vibration became sound. Sound slowly became words.

But they weren't words she was able to recognize.

"Ka-nu eer-me?!"

She tried to blink but found that she didn't need to do that either. Instead, she simply gazed up into the abyss, listening curiously as her ears came back to life. Someone was shouting. Someone seemed very anxious indeed. She just couldn't get it to make sense.

"Ang-on!"

The world was getting lighter. A great weight was lifting off her chest. One she hadn't realized was there in the first place. First the black lightened to grey, then the grey was tinged with dots of white. Those dots got brighter and brighter until they were burning into Katerina's eyes.

A sharp pain burst through her chest, followed by a rush of cold as the last of the snow cleared away and she found herself looking up into Dylan's eyes.

"Honey?!"

Honey? Crap—maybe I'm dead after all.

The world blinked back into focus just as he threw his body into the snow. His hands may have been urgent, but they handled her like she was made of glass as he swept her legs out from under her and fished her up out of the deep ravine.

She tried to help. She tried to get a foothold on the icy bank, or at least wrap her tired arms around his neck. But it was no use. He may have brought her back up to the land of the living, but a part of her was still down there. Hibernating in the ice.

"I can't believe it!" The second they were back on solid ground, he embraced her without a second thought. "You're alive!"

That's debatable...

Katerina blinked slowly. Allowing herself to be fawned over. Allowing herself to be held. The world was moving a bit too fast for her to keep up with, and the most she was able to do was simply lay there and wait to catch up. It took her a full minute to realize that Dylan was naked.

"Why aren't you wearing any pants?"

They were the first words she'd said since resurrecting and, in hindsight, she felt as though they should have been more significant. Wiser. Like her near-death experience had prompted her to discover some deeper meaning. But nope. He was naked, and she wanted to know why.

He glanced down self-consciously and quickly shifted her to the side, grasping for his clothes while keeping a firm hand on her. "I had to shift to get you out of there," he mumbled, yanking his pants up around his waist. "Wolves dig faster than people."

Sure enough, there were giant claw marks surrounding the hole she'd just come out of. A frantic display of both raw power and sheer panic had broken her free of the ice. It was a combination she still saw shining in his eyes as he gazed down at her, cradling her gently in his lap.

"Are you all right? How are you feeling?"

Her eyes locked onto his lips, still trying to slow things down. She felt like there was a question in there somewhere, but she was too dazed to hear it. He seemed to sense her plight and leaned immediately closer, speaking slowly in soft, gentle tones.

"What hurts?"

This time, the question got through. She considered it, thought-fully stretching out each limb while her cheek rested lightly against his bare chest. There should have been breaks. There should have been sprains. There should have been massive internal bleeding. But, strange-ly enough, minus an unprecedented level of disorientation, she seemed to be all right.

"Um...nothing." She could hardly believe it herself. "Is that bad?"

She wasn't paralyzed, was she? She'd actually moved all those limbs she'd stretched, right?

"It's a miracle," Dylan murmured in amazement. He helped her into a delicate sitting position, then ran his hands gently over both arms, both legs. Down her sides, up her back. Rotating her head back and forth as he checked her pupils. Nothing. She was just fine. "A freakin' miracle."

His own salvation had not been quite so astounding. The entire left side of his face had been torn open, like he'd been thrown into a jagged wall. There were hundreds of cuts and scrapes and abrasions covering every inch of visible skin and, judging by the tender way he was han-dling his shoulder, the thing had been ripped clean out of its socket.

But he was alive. They both were. At least for the time being.

But what about the others?

The second she thought the words, they heard a muffled groan. A hand popped out of the ice, followed immediately by a head of cinnamon hair.

"Tanya!"

Dylan propped Katerina gently on the snow and raced over to help. The tiny girl wrapped her arms around his neck, and then screamed in pain as her legs were tugged free of the ice.

"My knee," she panted, doubled over at the waist. "I think I broke it."

"We'll fix it," Dylan assured her quickly, wrapping his belt around it as a temporary brace before packing that brace with snow. The cold would numb her until other arrangements were made. In a flash, he made a cursory check for any other damages, then took her face firmly in his hands. "It's just a knee—we'll fix it. But Tanya, right now, I need you to think. Where's Cassiel?"

Katerina's head whipped around, frantically scanning the surrounding landscape. There wasn't much to go on. The entire world had been wiped clean, blanketed in a fresh layer of dazzling white snow. There wasn't a fae in sight.

"CASS!" she shouted at the top of her lungs.

Nothing.

Dylan clearly wanted to be shouting, too. In fact, a part of him was in a full-on panic. His best friend was missing, with limited air, and he hadn't the faintest idea where to start looking for him. The only thing he had to go off was a single witness. One who was half-blinded by pain.

"Tanya, please," he begged, "focus for me. You were with him last. Both of you were braced against the back of the cave. What happened next? Did you see what happened?"

Her head slowly lifted as she looked back at the boulder—buried in over twenty feet of ice. An almost dreamy look flitted across her face as she pulled the memories deep from within her dizzy subconscious, dragging them forth into the light.

"He never left..."

Dylan shook her shoulders. A little harder than he meant.

"What does that mean?"

She blinked quickly back to the present, trying desperately to summon her wits. "He shielded me from the worst of it, then got thrown into the ceiling when the ground shook. I was thrown clear, but the whole thing got buried after that. He couldn't have left."

That was all Dylan needed to hear. A second later, he was tearing towards the boulder, the very top of which was only barely visible over the sea of white. The air around him shimmered, and a second later a giant wolf was standing in his place, digging frantically through the snow.

Katerina covered her mouth as icy tears slipped down her face, while Tanya dragged herself closer, her dilated eyes locked fiercely upon the ever-growing hole. When it got big enough, Dylan shifted back into a man and slipped inside, falling noiselessly into the abyss. No idea whether his friend was even alive to save. No idea of how he was going to get back out.

"Dylan!" Katerina shouted, even though she knew it was useless. He was down there already, there was nothing more to be done. Still, that didn't stop her and Tanya from shouting at the top of their lungs.

"Dylan!"

"Cass!"

They waited for what felt like an eternity, each second more excruciating than the next, then Katerina sucked in a breath as a sudden movement caught her eye.

"THERE!"

An explosion of ice burst into the air, and the next second two heads of hair popped out of the snow. One was conscious and moving. The other was not.

The princess scrambled to her feet, shocked that her legs were still working. Fast as she could, she made her way across the ice and fell to Dylan's side, helping him drag the sleeping fae out of the darkness and into the light.

It was then that she paused, staring down in horror.

Cassiel had been perfectly cordial to her in the beginning, but since finding out that she was a Damaris that spirit had significantly cooled. He was still polite to a fault, but there was a distance between them that couldn't be breached. A civility that never seemed to extend to friendship. It was his choice, not hers, but under the circumstances she didn't see what could be done.

Because the two didn't talk much, she'd watched him instead.

Over the course of the last week, she'd seen him laughing and relaxed. She'd seen him tired, but patient. Wary, but charming. She'd seen Dylan, the strongest man she'd ever met, lean on him many times. He was a beautiful as he was strong. As intimidating as he could be kind. She'd seen a hundred different emotions, and a hundred different faces.

But never would she have imagined he could look like this.

Those beautiful eyes of his were closed. That invincible body was helpless and broken, as vulnerable as a little child. A dark cloud of bruises had laced its way over his fair skin, and although she couldn't see where it was coming from his silver shirt was stained with blood. He was breathing, faintly, but every breath seemed to come with the greatest effort, and when Dylan lowered an ear to his chest for a better listen, his face paled with fear.

"Cass." He shook him very gently, careful not to disturb his spine. "Cass. Wake up."

The girls huddled closer together as Cassiel lay perfectly still upon the snow. The tranquil look on his face stood in sharp contrast to the brutal devastation of the rest of his body, and even in the few seconds he'd been lying there that stain of blood had spread to the surrounding snow.

"What's wrong with him?" Tanya whispered, staring down with grief-stricken eyes. The two might delight in tormenting the other, but they'd grown closer than either was prepared to admit. In spite of her shattered knee she knelt down in the snow, gently taking his hand.

"Internal bleeding." Dylan looked like he could hardly say the words. "Most of his ribs are fractured; it sounds like one of them pierced his lungs. I don't..." He trailed off helplessly, trembling slightly with the cold. "I don't know what to do."

For a moment, everyone was silent. Then Katerina whipped off her cloak and lay it across the fae. Her hand reached out to Dylan, while she kept her eyes fixed on Cassiel's face.

"Give me your knife."

Dylan froze for a moment in surprise, then his face paled in horror. "Kat, you're not going to kill him! We can think of another way! There has to be something we can—"

"I'm not going to kill him," she said calmly, never taking her eyes off his face. "I'm going to save him. And to do that, I need your knife."

About five years ago, the palace had emptied as the royal family embarked upon their annual hunt. Normally, when hunting, the royal family extended only to the men. The king and the prince would set off with a contingent of favorite courtiers and guards, while Katerina and the rest of the women were left at home. But five years ago, after weeks of begging, the princess had finally been allowed to come along.

She remembered how excited she'd been as the grooms saddled up her horse and she rode out with the rest of the men into the forest. She remembered how exhilarating it had been to gallop full speed through the woods. The wind in her hair. The sun in her eyes. Leading the charge.

She remembered how abruptly terrified she'd been when one of the men suddenly fell off his horse and tumbled headfirst into the ravine.

The entire party had come to a screeching halt. People were shouting. The man was bleeding uncontrollably. The doctor had been left behind at the palace. For what felt like a small eternity, the man lay dying on the ground while everyone else anxiously hovered, wringing their hands helplessly as they desperately debated what to do. Then one man stepped forward. A young lieutenant, new to the palace, that Katerina had seen only a few times before.

Unlike the panicked people around him, this man kept his head. With nothing more than skilled efficiency, he knelt to the ground and tore open the man's shirt. A second later, he slipped his knife strategically between his ribs. The king had shouted. Katerina clapped her hand over her eyes.

But then the strangest thing happened. The man on the ground woke up.

"Your knife, Dylan," Katerina said again, sweeping her hair into an efficient knot behind her head. "He's running out of time."

After a moment of profound hesitation, Dylan reached into his belt and pulled out his trusted blade. He turned it over nervously in his hands before placing it cautiously in hers. She took it without looking and rolled up the hem of Cassiel's shirt.

His injuries were even worse up close.

By the looks of things, he'd been literally crushed against the wall of the cave. The jagged rocks had lacerated wide gashes of skin, but it was the internal damage that was the most pressing. It was there that Katerina focused her attention.

With the utmost care, she moved her fingers up the edge of his ribcage. Counting silently as she went. Mimicking the same motions she'd seen the lieutenant do all those years ago. When she reached the proper place, she pulled in a deep breath and pressed the tip of the blade to his skin.

...which is right when all hell broke loose.

"Are you crazy?!" Tanya shouted. At the same time, Dylan's hand shot out involuntarily and grabbed her by the wrist, stopping the blade in its tracks.

As she looked up at them slowly, shaken to the core, she was suddenly reminded that the four of them hadn't known each other very long. They had bonded as well as possible under the circumstances, but in the grand scheme of things they were still relative strangers.

And strangers didn't let strangers go poking their friends with knives.

"I can't..." Dylan's voice shook as he stared down at Cassiel's face. His pale skin was now tinted with the faintest traces of blue. "I can't let you..."

It was a turning point. The second she was needed the scared little princess disappeared, and a fearless young woman rose up in her place. Like flipping a switch all the tension left Katerina's body, and she gazed steadily into his eyes. Her panic was replaced with sympathy. The wild nerves gave way to calm assurance. A royal authority that was impossible to ignore.

"*Dylan.*" Her hands were sure, and her voice was steady. "Trust me."

Their eyes locked again, and he pulled in another deep breath. He had no reason to do so. In fact, he had every reason *not* to. But, for whatever reason...he did.

A second later, he released her wrist. A second after that, the blade slid into Cassiel's chest.

There was a rush of blood, followed by painful moan. Another rush of blood, and there was a sudden gasp as the pressure released and Cassiel was able to pull in a breath of air. His eyes shot open a moment later, flying around wildly before coming to rest on the girl kneeling in front of him.

"You..." he gasped weakly, hands coming up to his chest. "What are you..."

"It's all right." Dylan knelt quickly beside him, slipping a hand behind his head as he placed pressure against the wound. "You couldn't breathe, but Kat...she helped you."

There was a newfound deference in the way he said the words, and his eyes rested upon her like it was a favor he would not soon forget.

As for Cassiel, it was hard to tell how much he was absorbing and how much was lost in shock. His eyes travelled to Katerina when Dylan said her name, then returned almost immediately to the gaping hole in his chest. They widened slightly, tight with pain, but only a moment after that they came to rest upon something else. A trivial detail, but one that had a lasting effect.

"You gave me your cloak."

The others glanced down in surprise. Katerina had completely forgotten about the gesture. It had been pure instinct. To protect the fallen. To safeguard the weak. She hadn't thought anything of it until she saw the look of wonder in Cassiel's dark eyes.

"Of course I did," she answered self-consciously. "You'd do the same for me."

Maybe that was true. Maybe not. But one thing was for sure. The fae was looking at the princess as if he'd never really seen her before that day.

Of course, their resident shape shifter couldn't help but shatter the touching moment.

"So, what now?"

Since it was clear that their fourth member would survive the day, she had turned her focus to more immediate problems. They were still stranded in the middle of nowhere, in below-freezing temperatures, with a crush victim and a girl with a broken leg. Where did that leave them?

Dylan wiped his dagger on the fallen snow before pushing to his feet. His ice-blue eyes pierced through the stormy clouds with fresh determination as he glared up at the sky.

"Now we get off this bloody mountain."

Chapter 6

One of the strange things about travelling around with a ranger is that you don't need a map. Dylan *was* the map. Every step the others took for granted, every passing landmark, they were ingrained in his very bones. So, when Dylan was faced with the impossible question of how to get them off the stormy mountain, he answered the only way he knew how.

"We can't go forward, and we can't go back. But we can go around." He turned suddenly towards the east, a direction they'd been moving parallel to thus far. "Redfern Peak. If we can make it that far, we can bypass the worst of the storm and come down on the other side of the mountain."

"Redfern *Peak*?" Katerina repeated, stressing the last word. The snow around them was already stained with blood. Did he really think they'd be scaling mountains anytime soon?

Dylan read her concerns and answered them with quick assurance. "We're already at the top of the peak. We're not going to be hiking up-hill anymore." He hesitated suddenly, glancing down at his friend. "But it is a tricky climb down..."

Cassiel paled slightly at the thought but put a bracing hand against his chest and pushed shakily to his feet. Fae didn't heal the same way mortals did. They had a higher tolerance for pain and a greater natural endurance. As long as his strength held, he could make it to the peak. What happened when he got there, however, would be anyone's guess.

64

Dylan's lips twitched up in the faintest of smiles as he looked his friend up and down. "You up for something like that?"

Even bloodied and broken, Cassiel still managed to look so haughty it was all Katerina could do not to laugh. "You insult me," he scoffed. "I'll manage it better than you."

"I was just asking—"

"Put on some bloody pants, my friend."

For the second time, Dylan tightened the cloak that was wrapped around his naked body and hurried back to the boulder to recover the clothes he'd lost as a wolf. His ability to shift might have saved the day, but it left the rules of propriety far behind them.

Katerina cast a quick glance at the others before hurrying after him.

What she was going to say, she didn't know. What there *was* to say, she had no idea. But with the world spinning past them at speeds too fast to control, she needed something steady. "So...Redfern Peak, huh?"

He glanced over his shoulder, his shirt halfway above his head. "Princess, if you'd like to see me naked, all you have to do is ask. I am a loyal subject, after all."

Right. She could just picture this guy sitting down to pay his taxes.

She tried valiantly to smile but found herself quite at the mercy of her emotions. Instead of flashing a conspiratorial grin, as she'd intended, her eyes filled with sudden tears. Each one of them freezing before they could make it even halfway down her face.

"Kat?"

Dylan glanced back again, waiting for some sort of response, then stopped what he was doing the second he saw her face. The shirt was forgotten. The girl became his immediate priority.

"Hey." He gathered her up in his arms, ignoring the cold, ignoring the pain. Ignoring everything except her tears. "Honey, please don't cry. It's all right."

Honey, again. The man uses pet names when he's nervous.

"I'm sorry." She wiped her face, embarrassed, trying to get herself under control, but it wasn't the easiest thing to do. "I just can't believe what just...I mean, one second we were just standing there, and then..." A belated shiver shook her entire body as she pulled in a trembling breath. "When I woke up in the snow...I thought maybe I was dead."

Saying the words aloud didn't help like she thought it would. In fact, it made everything much, much worse. How was this her life? How were these her problems? Where was her palace, her horse, her bed, and her friends? Why the hell was she standing on this frozen mountain?

Dylan froze for a moment, then his arms tightened. "I know," he soothed quietly, stroking her fiery hair with one hand, while the other held her tight against his chest. "I did, too."

His heartbeat was faster than normal. She could feel it even through her clothes. Probably from the cold, the pain, and the adrenaline. He was still bleeding freely down his neck.

"But we're all okay." He clung to the words like a life raft. A man desperate to keep his head above the waves. But it wasn't enough just to save himself. He wouldn't stop until he'd saved her as well. "Hey! A *mountain* fell, and we're still standing. That counts for something, right?"

Yep, those things didn't sound any better when they were said out loud. But his smile was contagious. It wasn't long before the tears stopped, and her face relaxed into a reluctant grin.

"We're okay," he said again. Firm, this time. As if he was convincing himself as well. "It's over now. It's over, and we're all going to be okay. I promise."

They were kind words, but Katerina couldn't see how they could possibly be true. The four of them were stuck at the top of the world with no food, no shelter, massive injuries, and half the royal army on their trail. Their original plan to stay off the grid had just been thwarted by a fucking avalanche, and the dark storm above them was churning with an almost unnatural momentum.

Still...it was easier to lie.

"Yeah," she whispered softly, pressing her face into his skin, "I know."

That was the last either of them spoke for a long time. Flurries of ice and snow danced around them. Swirling clouds of white, with occasional crimson stains. It tangled their hair and caught in their lashes. Like being trapped in a beautiful but deadly snow globe. For a while, they just stood there. For a while, it was quiet. And for a fleeting moment, they were able to find some peace.

Neither one of them was used to such dependence. Neither one of them was used to the quiet comfort of placing themselves in someone else's arms. But for a split-second, standing there in the swirling snow, they let themselves succumb and simply held each other. Skin to skin. Cheek to cheek. Just two people standing at the top of the world, waiting for whatever came next.

"If you two are finished groping, let me remind you...*I broke my freakin' leg*."

Correct that. Four people.

And apparently the others were tired of waiting.

Dylan's shoulders stiffened, and he pressed his forehead against Katerina's hair with the softest sigh. He didn't believe his quiet reassurances any more than she did. But what else could they do but say them? What else could they do but make promises they might never be able to keep?

He held her another moment before pulling back to study her face with a forced smile. "So...you have anything you want to tell me?"

She stared back in surprise, blinking in the cold. "Like what?"

The smile grew genuine as flicker of curiosity danced through his eyes. "Like how you were able to survive a glacial avalanche without even a scratch?"

Oh...that.

Her lips parted uncertainly to answer, but there was nothing to say. It was a damn good question. A question that would no doubt haunt her every step in the days to come. But for right now, they had bigger things to worry about. For right now, it was a question for another time.

"Just lucky, I guess."

A flash of lightning ripped through the sky, and for a moment they froze perfectly still.

"*Yeah.*" Dylan laughed humorlessly as his eyes drifted up to the darkening clouds, growing more and more worried with each passing moment. "If there's one thing we are...it's lucky."

IT WAS ONE THING TO verbally commit to reaching a hypothetical peak. It was another thing entirely to get there. Especially after just having dug your way out of an avalanche.

The journey was as backbreaking as it was brutal.

Out of the four friends, only two could walk. One of the remaining two had a severe concussion and a dislocated shoulder, while the other had about ninety pounds to her name and was doing her very best to drag a shape shifter through the piling snow.

"How you doing, Tanya?" Dylan called after about thirty minutes of silence. The others were keeping quiet to preserve what little energy they had left, but he seemed determined not only to lead the way but to rally on the others as well. "Is that brace holding up?"

Tanya's delicate little pixie face twisted with dark sarcasm. "Oh, it's just *great*. You know, some people with shattered bones might prefer an *actual* brace, but not me. I always go for a belt."

The leather strap around her knee had begun leaking over with blood. Still, she shuffled onwards. Clinging to the side of Katerina's neck for support.

"That's the spirit."

He said nothing to encourage the fae. There was a good chance Cassiel would punch him in the face if he tried. But he kept a firm arm wrapped around him every step of the way, taking almost all his weight as the haggard foursome made their way slowly to the peak.

Hours passed. Each one stretching into the next. The storm raged on, beating down upon the four weary travelers trudging painfully across the frozen plain.

It wasn't long before Tanya called for a break. Katerina called for one not long after. Cassiel would rather die than show a hint of weakness, but when it became clear that he'd lost more blood than he had left Dylan called for one himself, and the four of them collapsed upon the snow.

"Not exactly what you had in mind, huh?" Dylan shot Cassiel a quick grin, taking the opportunity to examine him in the process. "When I came and got you from the hotel?"

The fae's already-pale skin had not a hint of color left. The ghostly alabaster stood in sharp contrast to the darkness of his eyes. Eyes that were still bright, despite being on the verge of defeat. "Which time?" he asked hoarsely, coughing halfway through. A faint smear of blood appeared on his lips, but he was determined to ignore it. "In Cambria? In Minsk? Or just a few days ago when you uprooted my life of whiskey and women and forced me to come on this little quest?"

The ranger sensed a trap and answered accordingly, unwilling to commit either way. "Both. None. All of the above."

The ghost of a grin flashed across Cassiel's face as he leaned back in the snow, stretching his legs painfully out in front of him. "Who needs whiskey? Or sex? Hand to the heart, I'd rather be here with you guys. Bleeding out on this god-forsaken rock."

Dylan nodded thoughtfully. "I'd rather you were here, too. It makes me look a lot more capable when you're all broken and pathetic."

"Can you hand me that knife?"

"This?" Dylan reached automatically for the blade, then froze suddenly, sliding it discreetly out of reach. "Uh, no. I don't think I will…"

Meanwhile, Tanya was too caught up in her own problems to worry much about anyone around her. "Is there any way we can make a fire?"

The men stopped threatening each other and stared down at her with matching looks of sympathy. Over the course of their travels, they'd broken countless bones themselves. They knew exactly how she was feeling. But, in this situation, there was nothing they could do to help.

"There isn't anything here to burn," Dylan said apologetically.

"What about your pants? You're never wearing them anyway."

Dylan's eyes narrowed, ready with a sarcastic reply, but Katerina was quick to intervene.

"What if we just set up camp for the night?"

The others looked at her in surprise. They hadn't considered this as an option. And, although the instinct was to reject the notion as long as the sun was still hanging in the sky, the suggestion made a good deal of sense. There was nothing but miles of snow as far as the eye could see. They were unlikely to come across anything they could use as shelter. And even the best of rangers could only go so long without a single landmark, before needing to rely upon the stars.

Not to mention, half their party was teetering on the edge of consciousness and sleep.

"Right here?" Dylan asked, but only out of habit. The more he looked around, the more he could see no better alternative. "It will be cold. *Very* cold, once the sun goes down. There's nothing we can use to block the wind."

"It's going to be cold anyway," Tanya replied, already yanking out a weathered blanket that had been strapped to her back. "Might as well get used to it."

Dylan considered it for another second, then nodded swiftly. Much to the relief of his companions, he removed the four tent pegs that were sheathed in his belt and tossed them on the snow in the middle of their little circle. They could rest. They had certainly earned it.

It took everyone gathered a full minute to realize the obvious question.

"Where's the tent?"

Dylan looked at Tanya. Tanya looked at Katerina. Katerina looked at Cassiel. And Cassiel stared back the way they'd just come.

"It was in my pack."

The pack that had been ripped from off him earlier that afternoon when an avalanche almost took his life. The pack that was buried beneath a mountain of snow.

For a moment, all was quiet. Then the fae pushed theatrically to his feet.

"No worries, I'll just run back and get it."

It was exactly what they needed to break the ice. Dylan stood up with a grin and helped him lie back down, checking briefly over his injuries in the process. Tanya snickered, and fished her trusty flask from her boot—one of the only things to have survived the storm. Katerina took the first gulp and felt it warm through her entire body, passing it on to Cassiel—who accepted it with a rare smile. The smile was returned with a tentative one of her own.

"So," Tanya started, squinting around the desolate landscape before her eyes came to rest on the solitary blanket, lying in the snow, "what are we going to do?"

All eyes turned to Dylan, who merely shrugged with a twinkling smile.

"We'll improvise."

LESS THAN TEN MINUTES later the four of them were lying on the ground, feeling somehow more uncertain than they had at any point during the storm. For the last few days they'd slept in closer quarters than this, but without the walls of the tent lending an air of acceptability the whole concept felt entirely different. It felt personal. Exposed.

It happened slowly. A hand here. An arm there. Legs wrapped around legs. Shifting casually closer to claim space beneath the same blanket. Anything for a little shared warmth. Anything to get away from the ghastly cold. With an eventual sigh Cassiel wrapped his arms around Tanya, holding the shifter protectively against his chest. She opened her mouth to instinctively protest, but he was incredibly delicate with her leg. So much so, that only a few seconds later she found herself cuddling closer. Lifting his arm and wrapping it around her shaking shoulders. Nestling as far back as was possible without getting blood on her clothes.

Kat watched them for a moment, then felt Dylan tense beside her. Braving the icy winds, she chanced a look over her shoulder to see his eyes glittering down at her in the dark.

They'd slept together like this once before. Why not do it again?

He got a little closer. Then so did she. Inch by inch, they moved together. Breath by silent breath. As the wind shrieked and screamed around them his arm circled around her waist, covering her with his heavy cloak in the process. Her back pressed up against his chest. Her slender legs tangled with his. At one point, there was a soft coughing sound as he spat out a mouthful of her crimson hair. She glanced guiltily over her shoulder, but he flashed her a boyish grin.

It was too dark to see much of anything, and the storm was too loud to hear. But they could still feel. Every warm breath against the back of her neck. Every steady beat of his heart. Every nervous twitch of his fingers as they buried tentatively in the folds of her dress, trying to stay warm.

It was intimate. It was public. And, given the combination, it was probably not their first choice. But in the end, the storm took that choice away from all of them. By the time exhaustion set in and sleep finally overtook them, the entire foursome was somehow intertwined.

Tanya's fingers were tucked into Katerina's sleeves. Cassiel had a secure grasp on them both. Katerina's fiery hair was flung across everyone present, and Dylan had stretched out his arm to grab the edge of Cassiel's cloak in his sleep—holding the entire group together.

They were still sleeping like that when the sun came up the next morning, reflecting off the frozen landscape in a dazzling array of blinding light.

The storm was over. The dawn had come.

Katerina was the first to wake up. Her eyes fluttered open, squinting groggily at the snowy plains. For a moment, she forgot entirely where she was. Then the events of the previous day came flooding back to her, and she felt Dylan's arm squeezing around her ribcage.

Her breath caught in her chest, and she froze perfectly still. Taking a silent moment to immortalize the scene in front of her. Never in her life would she have imagined such a diverse group of people. Never in her life would she have imagined that she might be one of them. That they would unite themselves to a common goal. That they would end up here. Together.

In a strange way, she found herself almost grateful for everything that had happened. As painful as it was, as downright devastating...it had led her to this very moment.

Then Tanya stretched out her arms with a sleepy yawn, smacking everyone in sight, and Cassiel jerked awake with a silent gasp. His lovely face tightened with exquisite pain as he looked down at the fresh stain of blood blossoming over his shirt. But instead of being angry, the way Katerina feared he might, he turned back to Tanya with an affectionate grin. Affectionate *and* exasperated, all at the same time.

Although the entire incident had happened without a sound Dylan's pulse quickened, and Katerina felt a hitch in his breathing. A second later he was awake as well, catching his friend's gaze with quiet concern, a worried question in his eyes. Cassiel rolled his eyes and gestured to Tanya, gently unwinding his legs from her own. There was another wince, followed by another silent profanity, but all in all he looked much better than he had the day before.

"Kat," Dylan whispered in her ear. Reluctant to wake her, but even more reluctant to keep her out in the open for even a second longer than he had to. "Sweetie, you need to—"

"I'm awake," she said quickly, squirming around to greet him head-on.

Big mistake.

He was much closer than she'd anticipated, and the second she turned around the two of them were nose to nose. Close enough to see every fleck of color in his eyes. Almost kissing.

He glanced up in surprise, then the corners of his lips twitched up as he tilted his head with a crooked smile. "Good morning."

A guilty blush spread across her cheeks as she scooted back into Tanya.

"M-morning," she stammered, painfully aware that Cassiel was only a few feet away. "Sorry, I didn't—"

"For shit's sake!"

There was a chorus of hacking coughs as Tanya fought her way through the princess' wavy hair, battling to the surface with a look of great resentment. She took a moment to get her bearings, but the second her eyes met Katerina's they narrowed with a not-so-subtle threat.

"Control that mane of yours, or I'm cutting it off."

Just like that, they came to the end of what had been a truly bizarre yet oddly tender night.

As the four of them set off once more towards the peak, stiff from the cold and wishing very much that they'd had something to eat for breakfast, they found themselves avoiding each other's eyes. Tanya couldn't help but blush every time she glanced over at Cassiel. Cassiel looked highly disconcerted to have fallen asleep with a threesome not of his choosing but seemed strangely touched by it as well. Katerina was filing everything away in her mind for later analysis. And Dylan?

As usual, Dylan was keeping his thoughts to himself.

But there was an extra spring in his step as the four of them set off over the snow. An extra twinkle in his eyes as he stuffed his hands deep in his pockets, whistling to himself with a little smile.

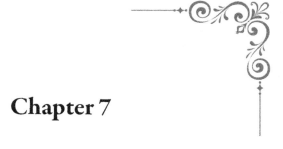

Chapter 7

Things were never quite the same after that morning.

It was a turning point. One that marked the beginnings of a new chapter. And while no one said it directly, everyone sensed the intangible shift. Like they'd all strayed across the same invisible line. And once crossed, there was no going back.

Not that anyone of them would want to. Quite the contrary.

They may have been limping, bloodied and broken across a frozen tundra, but Katerina could have sworn they were almost having a bit of fun.

"—at which point, I asked the proprietor to move me to a suite on the other side of the building. At least until they'd contained the beast and what was left of its hatchlings."

Katerina and Tanya were in stitches. Holding onto their sides, the pain was temporarily forgotten, and they plowed their way through the snow. Storytime was upon them. And Cassiel was so regal and refined, it was easy to forget that half of what he said was absolutely ridiculous.

"Enough—seriously!" Tanya doubled over at the waist and put her hands on her knees, laughing hysterically and flinching in pain at the same time. "I can't breathe!"

From what Katerina knew of the fae, they were supposed to be a reserved, dignified race of people. Older than men and gifted with immortality, they were said to have come from the magic of the stars. Children of nature who kept to themselves and took great care to avoid the toxic spread of cities and the troublesome affairs of men.

That's what she'd *heard*. Cassiel was a slightly different story.

...until the hatchlings were contained...

"Seven hells." Tanya grinned, still trying to compose herself as Cassiel swept past them with Dylan—looking like, for the life of him, he didn't understand what was possibly so funny. "How does he say crap like that, but still manage to come off like the prince of the forest creatures?"

Katerina stared after them with an incredulous smile. "I think it's because he *is* the prince of the forest creatures."

"I keep forgetting about that." The shifter paused, reevaluating for a moment, before continuing across the icy plain. There were landmarks in the distance now. A scattering of trees announced by the gradual thawing of snow. "Well, if that's the case, then how the heck did he end up bromancing around the five kingdoms with wolf-boy over there?"

Katerina shook her head curiously. Suddenly very eager to hear the answer to that herself. It certainly wasn't a likely pairing. A ranger and a fae. There was obvious affection there, buried *deep* down amidst a complicated history, but half the time she was surprised they hadn't killed each other years ago. Case in point. A few yards ahead of them, the men were lost to their own argument.

"The *beast*," Dylan scoffed, shaking his head with a grin. "The thing was a puppy."

His best friend might be on mile twelve with severe blood loss and a broken rib cage, but that didn't mean the two weren't still going blow for blow. Cassiel shot him a side-glare but seemed to expect nothing less. At any rate, he was more than up for the challenge.

"That just proves you were too drunk to remember what happened. The thing was more like an armored porpoise than anything else. It *swam* in with the tide."

Dylan shrugged dismissively. Enjoying himself far too much to be bothered with things like facts. "Some kind of aquatic puppy, then. The kind with gills."

"For bloody sake. Why do I even try with you—"

"It didn't help matters that you were wearing a dress."

"It *wasn't* a dress!" Cassiel threw up his hands in exasperation, ignoring the fresh stain of blood that followed. "For the last time—it was a ceremonial robe! Presented to me by the high chancellor of...*why are you smiling*?!"

"I missed you."

There was a brief pause, followed by a scathing glare.

"Screw off, Dylan."

Another pause. Then the fae shot him a look.

"...I missed you, too."

The girls shared a look. Thinking the same thing with a mischievous smile.

Bromance.

There weren't many provisions that had made it through the storm. More precisely, the gang had been left with nothing but a coat, a blanket, and a pile of tent pegs to a nonexistent tent. Tanya's lucky flask had long since been drained, and the fact that they were all walking around with half the usual blood and nothing but whiskey on an empty stomach was starting to catch up with them.

Katerina skipped lightly ahead and linked her arm through Dylan's with a playful smile. "So...this *wolf* thing..."

Dylan shifted uneasily as Cassiel's eyes danced with a wicked grin. "You mean, his canine problem?"

There was a beat of silence before Dylan gave his friend a humorless smile. "Cass, why don't you make sure Tanya's doing okay."

Cassiel started to refuse, but it wasn't exactly phrased as a question, and the look on Dylan's face was hard to ignore. Acting as though it was his idea to begin with, the fae swept gracefully back through the snow, leaving Dylan alone with the princess. Looking as nervous as she'd ever seen.

"My...wolf thing?" His lips twitched up, as though the phrasing amused him, before the smile gave way to nerves. "What about it?"

Katerina's mind raced as she wondered where to start.

Why hadn't he told her about it from the beginning? If they hadn't run into trouble, would it still be a secret? What the hell else was he keeping from her and, perhaps, most importantly—

"What's it like having claws?"

Dylan looked down at her in shock. She bit her lip and kept her eyes on the snow. *I'll admit...it wasn't my BEST question.*

"Claws?" It looked as though he was having a hard time deciding whether to laugh or simply stand there, aghast. "Are you...is that seriously your question?"

Instead of trying to get out of the hole, Katerina dug herself in further. "Well, I was going to ask what it was like having a tail, but it seemed somehow inappropriate."

This time, the laughter won out. A short burst echoed over the sparkling snow, vanishing tensions and lifting the hearts of everyone around him. She wondered if he knew he was able to do that. A second later, he turned to her again—an incredulous sort of wonder dancing in his eyes.

"How the heck are you a Damaris?"

The question caught her completely off guard. Just as much as her question had caught him.

It wasn't said with any sort of blame or malice. To be perfectly honest, there was a good chance he meant it to be rhetorical. But she felt the need to answer nonetheless. A need to defend the blood running through her veins. The same blood she was secretly coming to despise.

"Things weren't always..." She trailed off suddenly, staring out over the snow. "My father did some things he came to regret, but in the end he wasn't..." Again, she trailed off. Well aware that Dylan's piercing eyes were following her every move. "What I mean to say is—"

"I'm not asking you to hate your father," he said quietly.

Her eyes widened as she stared up at him in surprise. Her father had committed some of the greatest atrocities the world had ever seen. He'd hunted down the supernatural community to the point of extinction, and that community included Dylan. If there was anyone who deserved all that hatred—it was him. "You're not?"

Their eyes met, and a peculiar expression flickered across Dylan's face. One that settled into a sad, almost nostalgic smile. "He *died*, Kat. He was your father, and he died. That changes things."

It looked like there was more he wanted to say. It looked like the words were on the very tip of his tongue. But a second later, he was pacing through the snow once more.

"At least, it's supposed to..."

IT TOOK ANOTHER THREE hours to reach the peak. Another three hours but, given the state they were in, it felt like a small eternity. By the time they finally got there, even Dylan, who'd been doing his best to lift spirits, had settled into a quiet kind of gloom. Granted, it was a gloom that began shortly after he and Katerina exchanged words about her family.

"So, this is it?" Tanya shielded her eyes as she gazed out over the rocky cliff, taking in the extraordinary sunset painted across the horizon. "Doesn't look like much."

Cassiel nudged her playfully. "Some people would say the same thing about you."

It was true. The fae might look like some old world hero brought back to life, but no one would have expected so much from Tanya. Orphaned shape-shifters didn't really have much in terms of reputation, and the poor girl was nothing more than a waif.

But she'd survived an avalanche and trekked across the tundra. All on a broken leg.

"Well, those people are idiots," she snapped though, secretly, she looked rather pleased. "I'm a golden god. A champion amongst men. Mere flesh wounds cannot stop me—"

"That's good to know." Dylan came up behind them without cracking a smile. "Because it's a hard climb. And we've got to get going if we're going to make it down before nightfall."

For the first time, Tanya lowered her gaze to look *down* the cliff. Her bravado faded.

"Can't you guys just lower me to the bottom with a rope?"

Cassiel snorted and walked away, as Dylan's eyes lightened with that signature sarcasm. "The rope that we don't have? The rope that got lost with your pack?"

"Which got lost in a freakin' *avalanche*—"

"I'm not blaming you. I'm saying we don't have any rope."

"Well, you're a bloomin' *ranger*!" she retorted. "Give you a toothpick and a pocket watch, and you'll build a bloody colosseum! Can't you figure something out for *rope*?"

There was a pause.

"...you have a highly romanticized version of my profession."

Katerina came to stand in between them, peering cautiously over the edge. Sure enough, the cliff dropped down as far as the eye could see. Huge, jagged slabs of rock that clung together with no particular rhyme or reason, vanishing ominously into the mist. A mist that was already creeping up the granite mountain. Higher and higher as the sun began to fall.

"Dylan's right. We've got to hurry." She said the words only because she had to. In truth, she had no idea how the hell she was going to follow through. "The last thing we want is to get stuck halfway down with no torches when it suddenly gets dark."

The others glanced quickly over the side, thought better of it, then began securing their things. There wasn't much, but whatever they had was strapped firmly into their clothing. Katerina was just tightening the laces of her shoes when Dylan knelt beside her—under the guise of tightening his own. Their eyes met, and he flashed her the hint of a smile.

"You ever done something like this before?"

The princess blanched, then stalled for time. Looking deliberately down at her shoes. "Like this? Oh, sure. Loads of times."

This was coming from a girl too terrified of heights to jump off the one-story stable roof with the rest of her friends. She'd had to shimmy back across the tiles and take the stairs.

Dylan pursed his lips and nodded, keeping his eyes fixed on the ground. "Lots of rock-climbing days back at the castle, huh?"

"Oh yeah." Katerina paled even whiter, glancing once more into the plummeting abyss. "We earned merit badges and everything—"

"Don't do that," he said suddenly.

She looked up with a start, to see that he was standing right in front of her, his body angled strategically between herself and the cliff. No matter how hard she tried, she couldn't see the terror that waited just beyond. All she could see was that steady smile, those sparkling eyes.

"Don't look down. Always look at your hands." He spoke with the calm assurance of one who had done this kind of thing many times before. "You need to take a climb like this in pieces. One foot at a time. One hand after another. Break it down, and it'll be over before you know it."

She nodded swiftly, trying to project a lot more confidence than she actually felt. "Don't look down," she repeated, almost to herself. A torrent of wind whistled past her ears, streaming up over the side of the cliff. "Don't look down at the deadly, hundred-foot drop."

A wave of nausea started churning in her stomach, but before she could begin to properly panic a pair of warm hands closed around her own.

"The drop won't be beneath you," he said simply. "I will."

It was a testament to how much faith she had in his abilities that she was able to take some small degree of comfort in the words. But it was marginal at best. Yes, he might be climbing right below her. But didn't that just mean that she was going to take him down, too?

"You don't have to do that," she said half-heartedly. "Seriously, I should probably be the one to go first. That way, I can't cause any collateral damage."

"Not a chance." The words were firm, but he said them lightly. "Your safety is the highest priority here. And, at any rate, I fought hard for that spot."

Between the wind screeching in her ears, and the butterflies pounding away in her stomach, she was having a hard time keeping up with the conversation. But that last part struck her as a bit odd and she looked up in confusion, staring blankly at his enigmatic face.

"I don't understand." She shook her head, trying to get a cue from his expression. "You fought hard to climb down beneath me?"

For a split second, there was a crack in the façade. For a split-second, a mischievous grin broke through that unshakable air of calm.

"It might have something to do with the fact that you're wearing a dress."

Katerina blinked at him. Then blinked down at her dress. By the time it registered, and her mouth fell open with indignant rage, he was already moving away to give the others their instructions, glancing over his shoulder only once to shoot her a secret wink.

Absolutely shameless.

The plan was simple. Cassiel was going down first. As damaged as he might be, this sort of thing still came very naturally to him; As Dylan put it, if any of them were to slip they could use him to break the fall. Tanya was going to go next. Taking things as slowly as she needed to since she was only working with three limbs. Dylan was after Tanya, and Katerina would go last.

In a lot of ways, it was terrifying. *I could always just wait until they're all over the side, then take off running in the opposite direction. Pray to the gods of karma to send me some stairs.* But, in a lot more ways, it was oddly comforting as well. *They're all in this with me. We're all doing it together.*

Cassiel leapt over the side with no warning or preamble. Fractured ribcage or not, the man was born for this sort of adventure. Dylan shouted at him to watch his pace—an ironic warning to go slower than he was accustomed—before Tanya saluted them with a tight grin and vanished as well.

Just a few seconds later, it was just Dylan and Katerina. Standing together at the top of the cliff.

This is a bad idea, a really BAD idea. Of all the bad ideas we've had so far, this has to be the worst one.

"Shall we?"

She looked up from her fatalistic trance to see Dylan offering his hand. The blinding sunset was behind him, and for a second she completely forgot to be afraid.

It's a bad idea...but he'll be with me.

He flashed her an easy smile, gesturing gallantly to the edge of the cliff. It was a bizarrely chivalrous gesture, one that reminded her suddenly of the many handsome lords who'd helped her in and out of carriages, extending their arms with a charming smile.

"We shall."

Their eyes met for a fleeting moment. For a fleeting moment, time stood still. Then, without a word of warning, he leaned down and surprised her with a kiss. A kiss so sudden and passionate, it took her breath away. She was still recovering when he pulled back a second later.

He flashed her a smile. Gave her a little wink. Then leapt over the side of the cliff.

A second after that...she followed.

WHEN KATERINA LOOKED back later, trying to be as objective as she could, she still had no earthly idea how she'd managed the climb down Redfern Peak. It was worse than anything she could have possibly imagined. A literal nightmare come to life, pushing her to every emotional, physical, and psychological limit. Then it pushed her some more.

"You're doing great, Kat. Watch your grip."

She might be a princess with no experience in the ways of the world, tragically combined with no upper body strength, but even she was impressed that she hadn't yet tumbled off the cliff to face her inevitable doom. They'd been going at it for a little over twenty minutes and, according to Dylan, they were more than halfway down.

The end was almost in sight.

Of course, he'd been saying that for the last ten minutes. She was beginning to suspect him.

"Let me guess," she panted. "We're almost to the bottom, right? No need to lose hope?"

She didn't need to see his face to tell he was smiling. And she didn't need to see his eyes to spot the obvious lie. "That's right. Any minute now. Just keep on going. Slow and careful."

Thus far, she had stuck to his advice as well as she could. There had only been two times when she'd chanced a peek down into the ravine. The first time, she'd been met with a scathing glare and a twirl of Dylan's fingers—telling her to turn back around. The second time, she'd seen that his arms were shaking almost as much as her own.

When she tried a third time, not much had changed.

She couldn't see the others anymore. They were too far down in the mist. But she hadn't heard any screams yet, and she was taking that as a good sign. In fact, the only indication she'd had to know the others were struggling was the faint smear of blood she'd seen on one of the footholds a while back. Whether it was from Cassiel, or Dylan, or Tanya—she didn't know.

"So...tell me about life in the castle."

She startled in surprise, and almost lost her hold on the rocks. Fortunately, Dylan had been impeccable thus far, pointing out where to put her hands and feet, and she was able to get her grip almost instantaneously. "Excuse me?"

If he was straining, and by now he had to be, she'd never have been able to tell from the sound of his voice. It was just as calm as ever. Hardly even out of breath.

"You know...the balls, the gossip, the epic croquet matches. Tell me about it."

The world's most unlikely smile crept up the side of her face. "You want to know about the castle gossip, do you? Dylan Aires wants the inside scoop?"

"I'm dying to know."

She snorted under her breath. *I'll bet. Dying to distract me is more like it.* Still, it was a good strategy and she wracked her brain for something entertaining, trying to play along. "Well...there was the time that Lady Marchel drank too much wine at dinner and face-planted right in the middle of the cheese course. I was just two seats down. It wasn't pretty."

A soft echo of laughter drifted up from the rocks below. "I'll bet. What else?"

"Hmm..." She thought about it, forgetting entirely about her shaking arms, and aching fingers, and the deadly drop below. A second later, her face lit up with a happy memory. "A few years ago, at Christmas, Kailas and I decided to play a prank on our new tutor. You see, the man had a terrible fear of spiders, so on the night of the big feast, we snuck into his chambers and..."

She trailed off. Remembering each moment in excruciating detail. Remembering the exact look of breathless excitement that had lit up her brother's mischievous face.

Talking about Kailas was painful. She'd have to avoid doing it in the future.

"What else?" Dylan was careful not to let the quiet go on too long. As usual, he seemed to have a better read on her thoughts than she did. "What about suitors, marriage proposals—that sort of thing. You're eighteen years old. You must have had a lot of those."

By this point, Katerina was having trouble keeping it all straight. Was he still trying to distract her from the climb? Was he trying to move the conversation away from Kailas? Or was he asking about potential suitors, because the two of them had recently shared a perfect sunset kiss?

"There have been a few..." she answered coyly.

That produced a reaction. He might have been trying to distract her before, but it was clear from his sudden shift in tone that he was far more interested in the conversation than he'd let on.

"Oh, *really*." For a moment, she was half-convinced he was going to double back and join her, if only to interrogate her more thoroughly. "Do tell."

She bit down on her lip with a smile, cautiously navigating a dangerous foothold. "Let me give you a lesson in manners, Dylan Aires: a lady never tells."

There was a moment of silence. One in which both parties silently wondered what to say.

"Yeah...tell me anyway."

Katerina couldn't help but laugh. Direct as always. A man as straightforward and candid as Dylan would never make it in a royal court.

"Well, first there was Henry, the Duke of Allouve."

"...sounds like a prick."

"Then there was Alexi, Crown Prince of the Northern Realm."

"...I always thought he was a woman."

"But the one who was most persistent would have to be Matthew Lansbury, a knight in my father's kingdom. We grew up together."

"Lansbury..." There was a thoughtful pause as Dylan tried to place the name. "You mean from Esterworth Castle? Carl Lansbury's son?"

For the fourth time, Katerina glanced down. This time with a bit of a frown.

"How did you know that?"

There was an infinitesimal pause before that abrasive wall came back up.

"I'm not a peasant, you know. Some of us make it a point to keep up with the ins and outs of the monarchy. Especially when they're usually the people trying to kill us..."

Nice try. But you're not throwing me off that easily.

"I'm serious," she insisted. "How would you know that?"

"Why would you want to date his son—that's the real question."

"Who said I did? I said he's been persistent, that's all." By now, she had stopped and was staring down at him with a glare. He was staring right back up, just as defiant. "And just for the record, you've been persistent, too."

His eyebrows lifted slowly, with a self-assuredness she couldn't believe.

"You think this is persistent, what I've been doing? You think I've been giving this my all?"

Despite her precarious situation, she kept her cool. A feat she probably wouldn't have been able to do before she left the castle. "I think you keep kissing me with no provocation, then shifting into a dog and refusing to talk about it."

"...a wolf."

"Whatever."

He took a second to collect himself, ignoring the fact that he was dangling fifty feet above the ground, his lips twisted up into an arrogant smirk. "Honey, when I get persistent...IF I get persistent...you'll be the first to know."

A rush of blood heated her cheeks, but she kept her expression perfectly neutral. "Why does that sound like a threat?"

He laughed shortly, turning back to the rocks. "Because over half the people in this kingdom want to kill you right now. My guess is that everything sounds like a threat."

Why, that little—

"Do you really have to do that?!" she demanded furiously, lowering herself down another foot and wedging her foot into the slick granite. "Do you really have to say it like that?"

He looked up in surprise, accustomed only to a rougher kind of play. "Like what?"

"Oh, for bloody sake, Dylan!" She finally lost her temper, kicking a handful of loose pebbles down at his face. "I'm clinging to the side of a cliff, like some arthritic mountain goat who got severely lost, and you try to cheer me up by saying—"

"I'm not trying to cheer you up," he interrupted fiercely, blinking bits of stone and dust from his eyes. "It's not my job to cheer you up. It's my job to keep you safe, and to tell you the truth. Two things that have been severely lacking in your life as of late."

"Oh, that's great. Make fun of me." She rolled her eyes, trying her best to secure a foothold that was a few inches beyond her reach. "The royal army turned against me—*ha, ha, ha*. My brother sent his giant dogs into the woods to kill me—*ha, ha, ha!*"

Dylan was unamused by her banter, and he kept his attention focused only on her hands. "Don't try to stretch for that; find something closer."

It went in one ear and out the other. She reached her arm precariously across the rock. "You want to know something? At least Kailas is upfront about it," she continued, thinking about it for the first time. "He wants the throne, so he has to kill me. It's pretty straightforward."

"Kat, I'm serious—"

"Unlike you," she was almost there now, her fingers gripping against the wet stone, "the *truth-telling ranger* who's actually lied to me consistently since the moment we met—"

It happened before she realized it. Before she even had time to gasp. One second, she was holding onto the cliff like the others. The next, she was falling through the air.

The last thing she saw was the sky streaking out in front of her. A golden sunset stained with burnt crimson. Like blood dripping over a crown. The last sunset she'd ever see.

Chapter 8

It's funny, the things that come back to you in the end.

As she was falling, Katerina had a sudden memory of her first horse. A stallion so tall she'd had to walk up a stack of portable steps just to get on top of him. A second later, the face of her old piano teacher flashed before her eyes. A kind woman who'd slipped her secret sweets and candies whenever her governess wasn't looking. Then it was her mother.

This one was harder. No matter how many times she tried to picture the queen's exquisite face, she could never make it clear. She had a thousand memories, of course, but they tended to focus on a particular smell, a fleeting touch. The woman herself was always blurred.

But not today. Today, Katerina saw her in perfect clarity.

Fiery red hair. Stunning grey eyes. And a flawless, ivory-skinned face. A face that seemed destined to wear a crown. A face that looked remarkably like her own.

Funny, how those things come back to you. A moment before you'll never see them again.

"KAT!"

Her arms came up in slow motion. Her eyes fluttered shut. For a moment, all she felt was the wind in her hair and the cold chill of the mountain as she plummeted into the mist.

Then a hand caught her by the wrist. Snapping the bone in half.

A scream that was equal parts shock and pain ripped through her teeth as her body swung suddenly through the air, crashing into the jagged rocks once again. There was a moment where everything was lost to disorientation, and by the time she opened her eyes a strong arm had wrapped around her waist. Dylan was pinning her body to the mountain, using nothing but his own.

"Are you all right?!" he gasped, still reeling from the sight of it. "Katerina, are you all right?!"

She blinked a few times, very slowly. Her breath billowed out in a frosty cloud, and without thinking about it she pressed her forehead painfully against the rough stone.

"Honey, talk to me! Tell me that you're all right!"

She could feel his heart pounding through his shirt. His arms were shaking from the stress of the climb and the weight of holding them both, but she didn't worry for a second that she would fall. That fear was over. He had her now. She was safe.

"I'm all right," she whispered. *He called me honey again.*

"Say it again," he demanded. A part of him was dying to look her over and see for himself, but he was unable to move even an inch lest they both fall. "Kat, say it again. Convince me."

She wanted to reassure him. She really did. But she was in a daze. With her mother's face still twinkling before her eyes she twisted her head against the rock, staring at him in wonder. "You...you saved my life."

It wasn't the first time that it had happened, but it was no less staggering. The selfless way he'd thrown his body between her and the abyss. The complete lack of fear that propelled him forward. That moment of connection when their hands intertwined, when the terror subsided, and she knew, without a doubt, that she was going to live.

"You saved my life," she said again, trying to reaffirm it to herself. He didn't respond. He simply clung onto her in shock. Trying to slow things down. Trying to catch his breath. "Again."

For a moment, all was silent. Then a tentative voice echoed up from the abyss.

"Actually...not so much."

For the second time, Katerina stifled a little shriek. Dylan's arm tightened around her in alarm before the two of them twisted around, staring, dumbstruck, at the ground below.

With an almost comedic synchronicity, Cassiel and Tanya lifted their hands in an apologetic wave. The evening breeze was blowing the mist away, and it was suddenly easy to see that they were within easy jumping distance of the ground. Dangling off the cliff just a few feet above their friends' heads. Friends who were doing their very best not to smile.

Dylan's entire body wilted with a quiet curse as he pressed his face into the stone. "You've got to be bloody kidding me..."

"What was that?" Cassiel called cheerfully. His composure had lasted all of two seconds, and now he was grinning ear to ear. "It's crazy that I couldn't hear you, because you're actually *really close to the ground*."

Without another word, Dylan released his vise-like grip on Katerina. She landed lightly upon the forest floor, clutching her wrist and flushing seven shades of scarlet. Dylan landed beside her a second later, wearing a vicious scowl and refusing to look anyone in the eye.

"Not a word," he growled, knocking the fae hard in the shoulder as he swept past him into the trees. "Not a single word."

"Oh, I'd say the chances of that are pretty slim."

As for Tanya, it was taking everything she had not to recreate the epic moment right there on the spot. Only her broken leg kept her temporarily grounded. That, and the dark look of warning Katerina gave her the second she opened her mouth. In the end, she merely gestured to the trail.

"Well...shall we find somewhere to make camp?"

No one answered her. They all simply filed, one by one, into the forest. Some smiling, some glowering into the trees. Not one of them sparing a second glance at the mountain peak. Not one of them taking a single moment to acknowledge how much they'd risked, and how far they'd come.

Not that any of us is likely to forget...

Katerina lingered at the rear of the pack, stepping lightly over the blanket of pine needles and clutching discreetly at her fractured wrist. She hadn't even felt it in the moment. It hadn't been until the mist cleared and they'd landed that the stabbing pain broke through into reality.

It throbbed and ached as they wound their way through the emerald trees. The others might be used to such pain and such spectacle, but both were brand new for Katerina. Truth be told, she found herself a little overwhelmed. Sometimes staring up at the sun-streaked canopy, listening to the recurrent chorus of a thousand invisible birds. Sometimes marveling that she was even able to walk straight when one of her bones was cracked straight through the center. For a moment, she almost found herself wishing that her brother was there to see it for himself.

He'd always been the warrior, riding out into the sunrise, while she'd always been soft. The perfect little princess who stayed behind at the castle, sipping sparkling wine and sitting on silk cushions with her ladies. If only he could see her now. He wouldn't believe his eyes.

Then a twig snapped somewhere in the distance and she scurried back to the group.

No...I'm very glad Kailas CANNOT see me right now.

"How's the wrist?"

She glanced up in surprise to see Dylan standing right before her. Whether he'd abandoned his place in the front because he heard the noise as well, or if he'd simply been waiting for a chance to speak with her in private, she didn't know. As it stood, he was having trouble meeting her eyes.

"It's fine," she said quickly, stuffing it back into her sleeve and fighting the wince of pain that followed. "Just a little sore. No big deal."

He stared at her for a moment, delicately reaching for her hand. She immediately offered out the uninjured one and his lips twitched up with a faint grin as he reached for the other.

That grin was quick to fade.

"I'm sorry." He ran his fingers delicately over the skin as a look of true remorse clouded his handsome face. It was broken, all right. She could tell from the look in his eyes. "I thought we were so much higher...I never would have—"

"Would you stop?!" Katerina exclaimed. The words were a bit louder than she'd anticipated and the others stopped in their tracks, turning around curiously to listen in. "There was no way that you could have known, and that couldn't matter less! You risked *everything* to catch me! To *save* me!"

Tanya bit her lip with a mischievous grin. "From a deadly, ten-foot drop—"

"Shut up, Tanya!"

It would be a long time before Katerina was able to see the humor in the situation. And until such a time, she certainly wasn't going to let the others tease Dylan for a selfless act of sacrifice that most surely would have saved her life. Not if she could help it.

"I'm only agreeing with you," the shifter replied innocently.

"Well, stop." The dainty princess mimicked a hand gesture she'd seen the men make a hundred times, then twirled her fingers and pointed the others back to the path. "Dylan saved me, and that's the end of it. Now, let's find a place to make camp."

The others shared a quick grin as Dylan turned swiftly on his heel—eager to put as much distance between himself and the others as was humanly possible.

"I didn't do anything," he muttered as he headed off into the trees.

"Hey, that's not true," Cassiel called after him kindly. "You broke her wrist."

NEEDLESS TO SAY, BY the time the sun had set and the need to find shelter for the night had become desperate the collective mood had not improved. Tanya and Cassiel were still silently delighting in what had to have looked like the most anti-climactic 'rescue' in the history of the world, Dylan was still mortified and appalled to have done it, and Katerina was still nursing her hurt wrist.

To make matters worse, it started to rain...

"Well, that's just perfect," Tanya narrated in a loud, pitiful voice. "They survived the harrowing climb down the peak, only to drown in a monsoon shortly to follow."

"It came out of nowhere," Cassiel said softly, gazing out with a slight frown at the torrential downpour soaking the forest. "There wasn't a cloud in the sky."

"As far as luck goes, you have to admit that it's consistent," Katerina said helpfully.

Dylan shot her a reluctant grin before handing his blade to Cassiel and lifting himself effortlessly up the trunk of the nearest tree. He vanished for a moment, using the higher vantage point to scan the surrounding area, jumping back down with a plan.

"There's a small outcropping of rocks just half a mile east. Looks like they might provide a little shelter. Everything else around here is just trees."

"Sounds good to me," Katerina said with a shiver. At this point, anything that wasn't just 'standing out in the rain' sounded good to her. Already, it had soaked through her clothes and was trickling in freezing little rivulets down her spine. The others concurred.

They picked up speed and reached the rocks in only a few minutes. Dylan was right. They curved in such a way as to provide a bit of shelter for those gathered underneath. The only problem was, they weren't the only ones to have gathered.

At least ten other people were huddled beneath the giant stone seeking shelter from the rain. And 'people' was using the term rather loosely. Even from a distance, Katerina was able to see the telltale ears of a woodland sprite, as well as the sallow complexion of a rain-drenched vampire.

Great...more vampires. And I'm the only one not covered in some degree with blood.

The group pulled up short the second they saw the others, pausing with the caution of those who had the entire might of the royal army on their trail. For a minute, they all silently debated leaving. Then a flash of lightning shot through the sky, and they decided to take their chances.

With Dylan and Cassiel in the front they elbowed their way quickly to the back of the huddled masses, taking shelter in the back of the cave. They were clustered closely but casually, with one hand always at the ready. But Katerina wasn't worried. Their standoffish position alone was meant to dissuade any well-meaning introductions.

Of course, that always seemed to work better in theory...

"Ben Gold." A jovial man stuck his hand right under Dylan's nose the second the four of them had claimed space beside the others. "Pleasure to meet you. Despite this awful rain."

There was a slight pause, then Dylan accepted carefully. Instinctively wary of such an outgoing personality. "Riley O'Keathe, and these are my friends. And yeah," he glanced up at the roiling clouds, "it's a little intense. Came out of nowhere."

When the man followed his gaze, he leaned in for a casual sniff. So quick and discreet that no one else realized he'd done it. Katerina watched closely as his face relaxed: the possible threat was immediately downgraded. No, the man wasn't a shifter. No, he wasn't secretly armed with royal military supplies. Yes, there was a chance that he was exactly what he seemed.

A soggy old man. Taking shelter from the rain.

"Where are you from?" Dylan asked politely, shifting a little so the side of his face that had been torn up by the avalanche was hidden in shadows. "Is there a village nearby?"

Katerina fought back a grin. Of course, Dylan wasn't just being po-lite. Of course, he'd take advantage of every new introduction just to get the lay of the land. Always strategizing, that one.

"Not far." The man pointed out into the rain, squinting slightly, as though he could see it even through the trees. "If you keep following the river, it takes a turn about three miles down—"

"What about you, dear one?" Katerina jumped in her skin as an-other voice entered the conversation. One aimed solely at her. "Are you from the village as well?"

She looked down to see an old woman looking back up at her with a smile. A woman just as old as the man Dylan was talking to. Her first instinct was to protect her eyes, on the off chance she was a hag looking to claim them for shillings, but a second look calmed her nerves. No, this woman was no hag. In fact, everything about her looked reassur-ing. From her smile to her eyes, right down to the little flowers stuck in her lapel.

"No," Katerina said quickly, flashing an apologetic smile, "just pass-ing through."

The woman nodded sagely, gazing out into the trees. "I'm passing through as well. The plan was to head west, to the Festival of Woodland Lights, but the weather has delayed me so much, I fear by the time I ar-rive the entire celebration will be over."

Katerina perked up eagerly. It wasn't often that she stumbled across a shared point of reference in the supernatural world. She was quite de-lighted to capitalize upon it now.

"The Festival of Woodland Lights?" she asked excitedly. "We were just there. I spent a—"

"—fortune on hotel bills." There was a gust of air as Cassiel swept suddenly in between them. His bright eyes locked on the woman, and a firm hand locked around Katerina's arm. "What do you want, witch?"

What the—?!

"Cass, don't be rude!"

Katerina didn't know what surprised her more: The cold bluntness from her impeccably-mannered friend, or the protective grip on her arm. But the woman didn't seem at all perturbed. In fact, she seemed as though she was rather expecting it.

"He wasn't, dear one." She stepped back with a twinkling smile. "I am a witch. Gifted with a magic that would be only too obvious to a fae. I salute you, sir. For your instincts."

Cassiel nodded curtly but didn't relax his position. There was a natural animosity between those blessed with the magic of man and the magic of the stars. It was a centuries'-old tension, and by the looks of things it was still going strong today.

"What do you want?" he repeated bluntly. "Why are you speaking to her?"

A glimmer of frustration flashed in the witch's eyes, and Katerina blushed apologetically. But despite the coldness of her reception, she maintained a steady smile.

"I was merely making conversation." A flash of lightning ripped through the air as she raised her eyes to the storm. "We're all stuck here for a while, right?"

The lightning flashed again, and the fae relaxed his grip. A second later, Tanya called for his attention and he moved away, casting a final look of warning over his shoulder.

Katerina watched him go before turning back to the old woman. "I'm so sorry," she said quietly. "It was nothing personal, I promise you. We've all been travelling a very long way, and I'm afraid they're a little on edge—"

"No need to apologize," the witch dismissed her cheerfully. "I travel up and down this road quite often. A certain level of suspicion is to be expected." Her eyes flickered back to the fae, returning to Katerina with a smile. "Especially from someone as old as him."

The princess' eyes lit with sudden curiosity as she followed the woman's gaze. While she'd often wondered about the mysterious fourth member of their strange little alliance, she'd always been far too intimidated to ask. But maybe things had changed now. Since that night in the storm.

"At any rate, it's best you lot stick together," the witch concluded. "You can never be too careful in these parts."

The words caught Katerina's attention and she turned back in surprise. It was the exact same phrase Dylan had said to her back in the first village. The night he rescued her from the dwarves. A rush of warmth stirred in her chest, and she gave the woman a tentative smile.

"So why are you headed to the festival?" she asked politely.

It looked as though the witch had been waiting for her to ask. A look of extreme excitement came over her as she reached into her bag and pulled out a handful of multi-colored stones. The princess stared in open fascination. At a first glance, they didn't appear at all out of the ordinary. But upon closer inspection, they seemed to have a life of their own. A few were even glowing.

"What are they?" she asked curiously, reaching out a tentative hand. The closer she got, the brighter they glowed. Her eyes fixed on a purple one at the end.

The witch smiled knowingly, rattling them quietly in her hand.

"They're seeing stones. Drop them into water and they let you see anyone you like, even at a great distance. Only potent enough for two or three tries, but they always go over well at festivals."

Well, THAT'S certainly handy!

She wondered if they really worked, or if they were just a hoax to scam tourists. She knew what Cassiel would probably say. Either way, they were hypnotically beautiful.

"Here. Take one." The witch offered out the amethyst stone. The one that had caught Katerina's eye. It glowed even brighter the closer it got to her skin, and the princess almost took it on the spot.

"Oh, no, I couldn't," she said quickly, regretting it all the while. "That's a very sweet offer, but I don't have any money to pay you, and..."

...and my new friends would certainly not approve the idea of taking something for nothing.

"Nonsense." The witch pressed the stone into her hand. "Consider it a good luck gift. If this weather keeps up, we're going to need all the luck we can get."

She and Katerina shared a weary laugh but, as if on cue, the sudden downpour just as suddenly stopped. They looked up in wonder at the sky as the evening breeze blew away the last of the storm clouds, and the hint of a golden sunset flickered tentatively through the trees.

"Like I said," the woman clapped her on the shoulder with a jovial smile, and gathered up her things, "good luck."

"Yeah," Katerina murmured, turning the stone over in her hand, "must be."

Before she could say anything else, Dylan tapped her on the shoulder and cocked his head towards the trail. The rest of the people who had been gathered under the rocks had already begun to disperse, and Cassiel and Tanya were waiting on the forest path.

"Yeah, just a second." She slipped the stone into her pocket and turned quickly back to the friendly witch. "Well, it was nice meeting you, and thank you so much—"

But the woman was already gone. Lost in the bustle of the departing crowd. Katerina scanned around for a second, hoping to catch a glimpse of her threadbare dress or the greying, grizzled hair, but then Dylan called to her again and she headed out with the others.

The mood was significantly lighter now that the sun had returned. Between that, and the fact that they were soon going to turn in for the night, everyone's spirits were running very high.

So why did Katerina have a nagging feeling in the pit of her stomach? Why the strange hesitation gnawing away at her?

She smiled along with the others, laughing robotically at a random joke, but a second before they rounded the corner she turned and looked back at the rain-soaked little cave one last time.

The witch wasn't there. Not that she'd really expected her to be. All that remained was a pitch-black raven, perched upon a rock. The bird cocked its head the moment it saw her, watching her closely out of one eye. At the same time an inexplicable shiver rippled up the princess' arms, and she tightened her cloak instinctively around her.

A second later, the bird took flight. Katerina rounded the corner. The laughter continued as she and her friends tried to find a place dry enough that they could camp.

But she couldn't seem to shake that feeling. It followed her far into the night.

Chapter 9

Whenever the gang kept watch during the night, Katerina was always suspiciously left out of the rotation. It wasn't so much that they didn't trust her to spot danger, it was the question of what would happen if she did. The girl was sweet, but she didn't know how to fight. She was observant but hadn't been trained to know what to look for. And while her safety was the entire point of their little consortium, it didn't make much sense to let the others sleep while she kept a lookout.

In the beginning, she'd felt embarrassed to be left behind. Their second night together, when Cassiel had fought off a prowling cougar, she'd felt intensely relieved to have been safe in her bed the entire time. That night, she was beginning to feel restless, but it didn't have anything to do with not being chosen to keep watch. It was that same feeling again. The instinctual unease that had come over her the second she saw the raven.

She gazed up at the canopy of trees. Every now and then, between the branches, you were able to see the light of a star. A little speck of diamond dust, sprinkled across a shadowy blanket. She stared at each one in turn, breathing softly.

Back at the castle, it had been hard to see the stars. A steady rotation of guards, armed with blades and torches, constantly patrolled the perimeter, often stationing themselves directly below her window. The fire lit the night sky and made it difficult to see what might be shining above.

But it wasn't like that out here. Out here there wasn't a single ray of light, save for the dying embers of the fire and the silver of the moon. In the beginning, it had frightened her. Now, it was like a soothing balm. A peaceful sedative; one she found herself looking up at many times.

A slender arm flung suddenly across her neck, and she glanced down with a grin. Tanya wasn't the easiest sleeping companion but, despite her endless array of elbows and kicks, Katerina wouldn't have traded it for the world. Unlike the friends she'd had back at home, unlike even her beloved ladies—sworn to forever serve her—these people sleeping with her beneath the stars were different. They had the potential to become something more. To become family.

Tanya flipped again, striking the princess carelessly across the face.

...even if they leave a few scars along the way.

She grinned again and pushed herself up onto her elbows, letting her eyes slowly adjust to the darkness of the night. Another hand tightened automatically upon the edge of her cloak, and she glanced down to see that Cassiel had kept a careful grip on her, even in his sleep.

She pondered this as she gazed at his lovely face, flickering in the light of the dying fire.

He was a difficult person to figure out. When she'd first met him she'd written him off as nothing more than a frivolous playboy, too pretty for his own good. When he'd thrown that first punch at Dylan, she'd wondered at their history. When he'd walked away from his luxurious life without a second thought, to commit himself to their cause, she'd wondered at his character. And when he'd instinctively grabbed her, pulling her protectively away from a person he deemed a threat, she wondered what had changed.

Dylan had said he was one of the High Born. The closest thing the fae had to royalty. What she knew of the High Born was both tragic and brief. Dylan had also said he had a strong sense of honor, buried beneath that hard shell. It was something that was getting easier and easier to believe. The more time they spent together. The more those walls began to chip away.

She eased carefully out of his grip. Slow enough not to wake him. Tanya was a lot easier to evade, and a second later the princess was standing on her own two feet. There was one person missing from their party. But she had a pretty good idea how to find him.

"I'M RUNNING AWAY..."

The campfire was long behind her as she made her way through the woods. Hardly noticing which way she was moving as she twisted and turned through the dark trees.

"Back to the castle to face the music..."

There wasn't a sound in the forest around her. Just the occasional coo of a sleeping bird, or the rustle of leaves as a lingering breeze danced through the branches.

"Maybe I'll stop and see Bernie along the way. See if I can get some more of that soup—"

A hand flashed out of nowhere, spinning her around in her tracks.

"You think you're so clever, don't you?"

Her face warmed with an automatic smile as he stepped out of the trees. A smile that was reflected back at her tenfold. But they only ever lasted a moment. A second later, she twisted out of his grasp with a coy grin, swishing her dress back and forth as she pretended to consider. "Yes, I'd have to say that I am. I figured out that you're a shifter, didn't I?"

He pursed his lips. "You figured it out *after* I changed into a giant wolf...but, yeah. We'll say you're clever."

Without another word, he cocked his head to the side and she followed him to the place where he'd been standing, a little bluff overlooking the campsite and the woods. He dropped down to the rock with a grace that still shocked her and patted the place beside him. She sat down as well.

For a while, the two of them merely sat there. Staring up at the stars.

The lightning might have stopped, but the freakish weather continued. Streams that were supposed to be bubbling over were frozen still. Katerina's breath billowed out in a frosty cloud, yet a sprinkling of summer flowers was still blanketing the ground.

If it stuck her as strange, she could only imagine what Dylan was thinking. A ranger. A man who'd dedicated his life to living off the land. As they'd wound their way over the mountains and across the hills, she'd seen little flickers of it in his eyes. A lingering glance here. A trace of a frown there. Every day, weighted down with that same silent confusion.

"Couldn't sleep?" he finally asked.

She jerked out of her introspective trance and pulled in a deep breath. "After the second time Tanya smacked my nose, I figured I'd better walk it off."

Dylan laughed quietly, having suffered his fair share of late-night injuries himself. "Yeah, that girl's a menace." But his smile was soon to fade as he shifted towards her in the dark. "Speaking of injuries...how's your wrist?"

Katerina clutched it instinctively closer, as the pain she'd been trying to deliberately ignore pounded suddenly to the forefront of her mind. In truth, she didn't really know. She'd never had a broken bone before, so it was impossible to rank it on a scale. Shortly after the downpour had ended, Tanya had spotted a cluster of white flowers and tore off a few petals. After rinsing them with some rainwater, she handed them to Katerina and instructed her to chew them for a while before spitting them out. They'd help with the pain—she'd said.

Hyper-aware that the whole thing might be a prank the princess had followed her advice anyway, and much to her delight the pain did indeed subside. But the power of those petals was long gone, and little sparks of pain were shooting up her arm once more.

"It's fine," she said quickly. A little too quickly to be casual.

Dylan stared at her for a beat before his lips curved up with the faintest grin. "You know, you don't really lie well enough to be a politician."

She considered it for a moment, then nodded thoughtfully. "...that's probably why they chased me out of the castle."

There was a beat of silence, then Dylan burst out laughing again. It was such a warm sound, it literally seemed to brighten the forest around him. Katerina watched out of the corner of her eye, mesmerized, until he quieted down once more. Around the same time, his eyes fell upon her wrist.

"I really am sorry..." he started to say, then stopped himself with a quiet sigh. She'd already reprimanded him once for apologizing. He wasn't about to try it again. But he wasn't able to just let it go either. Like the princess, ever since it had happened he'd been playing it over and over again in his mind. "You know what's strange? You didn't even scream."

She turned to him in surprise, her long hair trailing down the side of her face. "What?"

"When you fell," he said again, staring deep into her eyes, "you didn't scream."

Yes, in hindsight, that was rather strange. Except that, to Katerina, it was the most natural thing in the world. She flashed a quick smile, looking back at the stars. "Of course, I didn't scream. I knew you'd catch me."

He stared at her a second more, unsure what to say, before he averted his eyes quickly and turned back to the forest. Some sort of nocturnal bird was singing a lonely song. A sad, haunting melody that lingered for a moment in the crisp air, fading quickly into the night.

"What's wrong?"

This time, it was Dylan's turn to be surprised. He glanced at her, unable to entirely hide the look of worry from his face. "Nothing. Why would you think something's wrong?"

She studied his face for a moment, flashing a sarcastic grin. "You know, you don't really lie well enough to be a ranger."

He chuckled softly. "Touché."

For a moment, it was quiet. He waited—hoping the question would simply pass. She also waited—silently pressing for an answer. In the end, it was he who caved.

"It's...this." His eyes roved over the shadowy landscape, growing more and more troubled with each pass. "I know this land. I've been here before. But this?" His lips thinned into a hard line, and he shook his head. "...this doesn't feel right."

Even a girl who had grown up in a castle could sense it, too. That same feeling of unease stirred again in Katerina's stomach as she hugged her knees, pulling them to her chest.

They'd done an incredible job thus far of evading the people who were after her. They'd beaten unspeakable odds just staying alive. Every decision had been carefully thought out, and every move was meticulously planned five steps in advance.

But, despite their every precaution, they had somehow veered off course.

The wind stirred up again, and without thinking Dylan slipped his arm around her tiny shoulders. She leaned into his chest, and together the two of them stared up at the sky.

Unable to shake the feeling that something was driving them forward. That something was taking them to places beyond their control.

IT TOOK AN AWFUL LOT to get Tanya out of bed in the morning, but the promise of a hot breakfast was enough to do the trick. Since losing what was left of their provisions in the avalanche, the gang had been collectively pretending that they weren't constantly starving. That they weren't swaying where they stood as the days of food deprivation and blood loss slowly took their toll.

But all of that was about to change. Sometime shortly before dawn, Dylan had tracked down a stag. How he'd done it with just his knife, no one knew. But Katerina suspected it had something to do with the large, wolf-like tears in the creature's flesh. However it happened, it couldn't matter less. The beast was hanging now over their fire, dripping deliciously onto the hissing logs as the smoke spiraled slowly into the sky.

"Aires, I take back every terrible thing I've ever said about you." Tanya wiped her mouth with her sleeve. "And trust me, there have been a lot."

Dylan chuckled, twirling a serrated bone between his fingers. The teasing banter was a lot easier to take in stride on a full stomach. As was the fact that at least three of them still had broken bones, and the fourth looked like he'd taken a battle axe to the side of the face. "Well, thanks for that. And don't let appearances fool you. I really invest a *lot* of time thinking about the things you have to say."

She tossed a bite of meat at him, laughing aloud when he caught it in his mouth.

"You two are like children," Cassiel said wearily, rubbing his eyes as the dancing flames reflected across his flaxen hair. "Like drunken children who were never taught to be still."

In terms of injuries, out of the four of them he was still definitely the worst off. The days of hard travel had done nothing to heal his wounds, and the subsequent nights of sleeping next to Tanya hadn't helped. The food had brought a bit of color to his face, but as things stood he was still tired and pale, wincing discreetly every time he shifted his weight or pulled in a breath.

Dylan took in every detail with a quick sweep of his eyes but fixed a careful smile on his face, moving swiftly around the fire so the two of them were sitting side by side. "Did someone have bad dreams?"

The fae shot him a strained glare, but otherwise ignored him.

"It was the one with the fish again, wasn't it? Tell me it was the one with the fish."

Katerina and Tanya fought back smiles as Cassiel's fingers twitched toward his blade.

"I thought so." Dylan shook his head with a sigh. "I don't know what to tell you, man. The context is strange enough, but when you throw in that bit with your father…"

Cassiel finally broke down and grinned. His dark eyes flickered up to Dylan's for a brief, communicative glance before he murmured something in a language Katerina didn't understand.

Dylan threw back his head with a laugh, kicking another log onto the fire. "What? The venison wasn't to your liking?"

"There was a claw in mine," Cassiel replied sardonically. "Missing one of yours?"

Dylan tilted his head with a sweet smile. "Aww, honey, you never complained about my cooking before."

"It usually involved a good deal of whiskey."

The entire campsite fell momentarily quiet at the word, like they'd taken a group sedative, then Dylan glanced suddenly towards the forest trail.

"On that note, my budding alcoholism isn't going to sustain itself. We're only half a day's walk from Fairport. It's just on the other side of the canyon. We can rest there for a little while and stock up on supplies. From there, it's just three days to Brookfield."

"Three days?" Katerina said in surprise. In her mind, the journey had been endless.

"Three days." Dylan flashed her a little smile before turning to the others. "Tanya, smoke the rest of the meat. We can eat what we want and sell the rest in the village. Cass, why don't you scout ahead for the best route to the canyon? From there, it should be an easy shot to the village." His eyes twinkled, and he couldn't help but add, "That is, unless you're too worn out."

Cassiel made a very particular hand gesture and disappeared into the trees, while Tanya got started with the fire. With nothing else to pack or prepare Katerina pushed slowly to her feet, staring off into the blinding sunrise.

Three days. We can make it three days, can't we?

The rain had stopped. The storm had passed. The sun was shining. And for the first time in what felt like years, they'd gotten to eat a hot meal. Their luck had changed, hadn't it?

Yes, she rubbed the stone in her pocket, *it most certainly has.*

She and the others headed off down the trail, all feeling the same way. Like an invisible weight had suddenly lifted. Like there had finally been a positive shift in the tide. Something to tip the scales back into their favor. They continued along that way for half a day's walk, thinking it over to themselves with secret smiles.

...until they got to the canyon.

Chapter 10

"OH—COME ON!"

Katerina wasn't sure she'd ever seen Dylan so angry. Not even when she'd wandered off on her own back at the festival. Not when he'd woken up with a concussion in a giant's cave. Not even when he was fighting for his life against a gang of vampires. This was much, much worse.

He literally fell to his knees with a vicious curse, glaring at the canyon beyond.

At least...it was supposed to be a canyon.

What the heck?

At some point, it had been filled to the brim with what looked like a massive landslide of rocks. The kind of rocks you couldn't climb. The kind of rocks you couldn't hope to move. In one fell swoop, their easy gateway to Brookfield had been sealed forever.

"What are the ODDS?!" Dylan continued to rage, his voice rocketing violently off the high canyon walls. "What are the freakin' odds? Are the gods against us? Like, seriously?!?! What have I done to deserve this?!"

The questions echoed back to him again and again. There was no answer.

"I don't understand," Cassiel murmured. He, too, had frozen dead in his tracks and was staring up at the colossus in utter disbelief. "How did this possibly happen?"

It was a fair question. Unless a mountain of boulders had literally dropped down from the sky, landing squarely in the canyon, Katerina didn't remotely understand what she was looking at.

"Limestone..." Tanya knelt down at the base of the nearest boulder, running a delicate hand along the edge. "Maybe the river swelled, and the villagers were trying to build a dam—"

"And they used *giants* to do it?!" Dylan pushed to his feet and stormed a couple of steps away, raking his hands manically through his hair. "No, I'll tell you what happened." His eyes flashed as he threw a look of pure murder to the sky. "Someone up there *hates* us!"

Give the man a target—he'd hit it every time. Give the man an opponent—you'd be sweeping the poor guy off the floor. But this was something different. Something you couldn't fight, or predict, or even see. Something that was rendering that invincible man completely helpless.

"SCREW OFF!"

His voice echoed around the canyon once more, rattling the stones, and sending a host of little shivers running up Katerina's arms. It was scary enough to see him lose control without the dramatic backdrop. If he wasn't careful, he was going to cause another rockslide.

"Hey," she put a tentative hand on his shoulder, trying to stop the manic pacing, "just take a breath. I know what this looks like, but it's going to be okay—"

"No, it isn't, princess!" He ripped his arm away, whirling around to face her for the first time. "None of this is going to be okay! None of us is going to be okay!"

Up close, he looked even worse than she'd thought. The bits of his skin that hadn't been ravaged by the avalanche had turned a frightening shade of white, and his fingers kept periodically flexing into fists—as if at any moment he might go and tear the boulders down, one by one.

"I've been charged with getting you to Brookfield. A task that's nearly impossible just by itself." He leaned in closer, enunciating every word. "My *entire job* here is to keep you safe, and if this kind of thing keeps..."

Words failed him, and he turned back to the mountain, staring up at it with the expression of one who was truly lost. Science had failed him. Geography had failed him. Almost two decades of gut instinct and experience were screaming at him to run the other way.

But he couldn't. They had to keep moving forward.

Somehow.

"We'll have to go around." Two deep breaths. That's all the time he needed to collect himself. Then the ranger was back, prying open a window as yet another door slammed shut in their face. "We'll just have to go around."

"There is no *around*," Cassiel replied quietly. His eyes never left the mountain. He didn't see Dylan's nervous glance. The way his face tightened with a preemptive apology.

"Yes, there is."

There was a moment of silence, then Cassiel rotated slowly with a look of dawning comprehension. Their eyes met, then he started shaking his head.

"Oh no, no, no, no. Absolutely not."

"What is it?" Katerina asked in alarm.

"*Absolutely not.* Dylan!"

The ranger sympathized, but in his mind there was clearly no other solution. The one road open to them had been closed. They would simply have to open another.

"It's the only way—" he began tentatively.

"NO!" Cassiel interrupted, as fierce as the princess had ever seen him. "We are NOT going to Laurelwood!"

JUST AN HOUR LATER, the gang was standing in front of a group of densely clustered trees.

They had been fighting through a strong headwind the entire hike over, but now that they'd arrived the air was suddenly still. Between that, and Cassiel's almost violent reluctance to coming, just peering into the emerald darkness was enough to give Katerina the creeps.

Laurelwood.

The princess knew very little, except what scraps she'd gleaned from obsessing over the castle's heavily-censored history books. It wasn't a subject that garnered much royal support, but throughout the years she'd managed to piece together the basics.

Before the Damaris dynasty had fought its way to power, the land of the five kingdoms had been ruled by the Fae. It was a different time, countless centuries before her generation was even born. The earth was younger. Wilder. Untamed. Yet beautiful and delicate all at the same time.

The Fae ruled with a different kind of magic than the sorcery her father had used to claim the throne. It was a magic derived from nature. An elemental magic. Katerina remembered Alwyn telling her about it once, when she was a very small child. Even then, she could tell he was jealous.

When the kingdoms fell, the magic died along with them. Living only inside those scattered Fae who had managed to survive. Lost in the tide of history. Fading from rumor into myth. It had retreated from all but a select few places in the world. Laurelwood was one of those places.

And suddenly, she was standing right at its doorstep.

The group stood there awkwardly for a moment, lined up shoulder to shoulder, before Tanya took it upon herself to break the stony silence.

"So...this is Laurelwood, huh?" she asked with a forced brightness. One look at Cassiel's scowl was enough to confirm. "It doesn't look haunted."

Uh...yeah, it does, actually.

"It isn't haunted," he muttered. "It's cursed. There's a difference."

Is there? Because they both sound pretty bad...

"It isn't haunted, and it isn't cursed." Dylan took the first brave step forward, motioning for the others to do the same. "That was over five hundred years ago, Cass. And even then, it was just a story told to scare away the Red Knight's army. You're really going to take it seriously?"

I think I'm taking it seriously...

"A curse is a curse." Cassiel's eyes flashed before he turned cautiously back to the forest. A quiet breeze was filtering now through the branches, making them whisper and dance. "I don't care how long ago it was...it's nothing to be taken lightly."

It was impossible not to be affected by the quiet words. Perhaps it was the weight with which he said them. Or the unfathomable look in his eyes. Perhaps it was the forest itself. The fact that it seemed to be reaching out with its branches, beckoning them inside.

Either way, they had no choice.

"There is no curse," Dylan repeated, soft but firm. "The villagers spread the rumor so that the royal forces would keep their distance—"

"What would you know?" Cassiel snapped. "You've been on this earth about five minutes, Dylan. All of you have. You know nothing of the way things were before."

For the second time in two days, Katerina studied him curiously. Wondering at his actual age. Wondering how the witch had been able to sense it. From the outside, he only looked to be about twenty years old. But the eyes gave it away. You could see centuries in those eyes.

It was an uneasy standoff. While the two men had a habit of being at each other's throats, they were almost always in line. But on this solitary point, Dylan could see no compromise.

"I know that if we don't cut through the forest, we're going to have to climb back *up* Redfern Peak, before hiking back over Clever's Pass. And, lest we forget, that entire entryway was recently blocked by a giant avalanche." He paused for a moment, his eyes asking forgiveness where his pride could not. "This is the only way, Cass. You know it."

Without another word, he walked deliberately inside the tree line. The girls paused a moment, looking between the two, before they followed suit. Only Cassiel remained behind. His feet frozen to the same spot. Staring at the forest like Dylan was asking him to walk through fire.

Fortunately, a willingness to walk through fire seemed to be a prerequisite to their friendship.

"You coming?" Dylan called without looking back.

Cassiel lingered there another moment, shivering slightly as he gazed up at the trees. Then he pulled in a deep breath and stepped over the threshold, following the others inside.

Curse or not, we're in it now. We're in it now...and there's no going back.

YOU KNOW THAT FEELING when you can tell you're having a dream? The colors are too bright, the world is too floaty? You try and try to wake yourself up, and when you finally manage to open your eyes it's only to realize that you're still dreaming?

That's what Laurelwood was like. A dream within a dream.

They ghosted noiselessly across the forest floor, moving with the instinctual silence one slips into when you enter a library. Even Tanya, the resident chatterbox, had the sense to hold her tongue. Instead, they kept their eyes sharp and their hands at the ready. What they were looking for, Katerina would never know. A nightmare come to life? An army of dead Fae? She was almost too afraid to wonder. But one look at Cassiel's face kept her moving, and it kept her quiet.

If he was this wound up himself, then she was on the verge of a heart attack. Jumping at every shadow. Startling at every sound.

Not that there were many. The place reminded her of a tomb.

"Why is it cursed?" she finally broke the silence to ask.

Dylan glanced back, looking wary, while Cassiel looked down at her in surprise.

"I'm sorry?"

"The curse." She cleared her throat, trying to make her voice sound stronger. "I know this place used to belong to the Fae, and they lost it in the Great War. So, who cursed it? And why?"

Dylan shot another uneasy look at Cassiel, turning back to the princess. "Kat, I'm not sure this is the best place to be discussing it," he began in a low undertone. "Maybe when we get to the other side—"

"Let her speak, Dylan," Cassiel interrupted, silencing him with a single look. "The girl deserves to know her own history. She is a Damaris, after all."

Katerina fought back a flinch at the way he said her name and gave him a tight smile instead. At least he was playing ball. And she couldn't stand the silence a second longer.

"This place did once belong to the Fae," he continued, glancing around at the trees. Even drenched in sunlight, there was something ominous about them. It was as though they were waiting for something. Trapped in a century long since passed, and unable to move on. "It was one of the last remaining strongholds during...what did you call it? The Great War?"

Katerina's face flushed as his lips twitched up in a faint smile.

"We learned to call it something else." What that was, he didn't say. He simply kept walking with a quiet sigh, his feet making not a single noise as they swept lightly over the ground. "In the final weeks of the war, the Fae army was divided. One was fighting in the north, another in the west, and the last was fighting right here in Laurelwood."

Suddenly, the eerie silence made sense. It might have happened half a thousand years ago, but Katerina shuddered to think of how many men and women had lost their lives in this very forest. How many had taken their last breath, gazing up at the ancient trees. She pulled her cloak tighter around her with a little shiver.

"The Fae were fighting well but they were heavily outnumbered, and the Red Knight had driven them deep into the woods." Cassiel was speaking in a flat monotone, as if part of him had been left back in time and all he was describing was playing out before his eyes. "Queen Eliea knew the cause was lost. The men had her troops surrounded and were closing in on all sides. In an act of supreme sacrifice, she went before the Red Knight and offered herself up instead. She surrendered her own life, that he might spare the lives of her people. The Red Knight agreed."

At this point in the story, Cassiel dropped his eyes to the forest floor. At the same time, Katerina's head shot up in confusion. She may not know as much about history as someone who had lived through it, but she knew a fair bit about the Red Knight. He was revered throughout the kingdom—her brother's childhood hero. And he wasn't exactly known for his merciful side.

"He did?" she asked in confusion. "He spared their lives?"

Cassiel's face tightened with an emotion that Katerina would never understand. Not if she was given seven lifetimes to try. He was quiet for a moment, then he shook his head.

"No. He didn't."

"The Red Knight tricked the queen," Dylan took over softly. "The second she surrendered her crown, he told his men to open fire. The Fae had already laid down their weapons. They were kneeling with their hands on their heads. It was a slaughter."

Quiet as it was, the word seemed to ring out in the forest, bringing the very trees to life with it. They bristled their branches and whipped out their leaves. Rising and falling in the angry wind.

"And what happened to the queen?" Katerina asked in a whisper. By this point, she was almost afraid to ask. She could tell by the looks on their faces it wasn't good. And knew enough about her own people to guess the ending for herself.

"The queen was killed as well." Cassiel pushed through his dark reverie and continued walking at a brisk pace. "The Red Knight kept her alive long enough to watch the massacre of her people, then he ran her through with his sword."

All in the name of the Damaris flag.

"But with her dying breath, the queen cried out a wicked curse." The fae's eyes flashed with muted triumph, and Katerina suddenly remembered there was another chapter to the story. "The Red Knight had won the day, but he would not live to see another. And if a child of man were to ever again set foot in this forest...he would not leave it alive."

I had to ask.

Katerina froze in place as a bone-chilling breeze rippled through the woods.

She remembered reading about the Red Knight with Kailas when they were kids. He had been a mighty warrior in the time of the Great War. The most distinguished and feared of all the king's champions. His campaigns had become the stuff of legends, and even today there wasn't a child in the five kingdoms who didn't grow up hearing his name.

But as epic as his rise to fame had been, it ended just as quickly. No one really knew what had happened. He simply never came back from the Great War.

The platoon he'd been commanding in the east left a trail of wreckage and broken bodies behind them, but when the king sent a messenger with his congratulations, there was nothing left to find. The messenger returned with gifts still in hand, saying that the Red Knight and his entire army had vanished into thin air. Never to be seen or heard from again.

Of course, the kingdom was wild with speculation. Many suspected disease. One foul pestilence that had wiped out the entire platoon. Still others theorized the men had fallen prey to the harshness of the land. Caught in a flash flood or wiped out in a blizzard. The wilderness on the outer rim of the kingdom was a savage place. Such things were not unheard of.

But standing there in the middle of the forest, listening to Cassiel's quiet words and the whisper of the trees, Katerina was suddenly certain of two things. The Red Knight and his men had never made it out of the forest. And she and her friends should never have come.

"So...what exactly are we doing here?"

It was impossible to keep the fear out of her voice, and Dylan cast her a quick glance before forcing a smile. "Oh, come on, you're telling me you believe in curses now?"

Both Tanya and Cassiel shot him a doubtful look, while Katerina rolled her eyes.

"In the last month alone, I've tripped through a ghost, sidestepped a hag who was trying to buy one of my eyes, and saw you change into what can only be described as a giant dog. So, yeah. My perspective on all things supernatural has changed somewhat."

Dylan scoffed, and opened his mouth to reply but was quickly interrupted.

"You don't believe in curses?" Tanya asked curiously.

He hesitated a moment, then compartmentalized and resolutely shook his head. "When I'm standing in the middle of what's alleged to be a 'cursed forest,' I choose not to believe in curses."

Her eyes cooled with a sarcastic smile. "And when you're not?"

There was a slight pause.

"I don't believe in curses."

But even as he said it, he cast a nervous glance around him and picked up the pace.

They continued like that for some time. Walking swiftly. Hardly talking. Hardly daring to look around. They had gotten to the forest a little after mid-day, and by Katerina's reckoning the sun should be close to setting. But, strangely enough, it stayed high in the trees. Never faltering or slipping lower in the sky. Like they were stuck in some kind of time loop. Trapped at high noon.

After several hours in the same fashion, she finally quickened her pace and caught up with Dylan. "What time do you think it is?" she asked softly, not daring to raise her voice.

He glanced up at the sky, his usual indicator, studied it for a moment, then lowered his eyes with forced determination back to the trees. "It's not that late. We haven't been in here too long."

Katerina's throbbing legs and aching belly begged to differ, but she chose not to press the matter any further. Instead, she focused on another. "Are we going to set up camp in here? Because I'd really rather—"

"Kat, we're going to get in and out of here as quickly as possible. You have my word." His eyes flashed quickly around the trees before he muttered under his breath, "I don't want to be in here anymore than you do."

A hundred more questions rose to the tip of her tongue, but she kept them purposely to herself. He was stressed enough as it was. And she doubted he had any answers.

Instead, she slowed back down, then fell into step beside Cassiel.

He hadn't said much since telling the story of the dead queen. It seemed to have taken a bit out of him just to say it. But while he seemed just as uneasy to be trespassing in the woods as the others, in a strange way he also looked very much at home.

The way he moved with an effortless grace through the trees. The way he didn't leave tracks like the others. The ranger in Dylan might have accustomed himself to a life spent in nature, but it was the birthright of every fae. A fundamental belonging that ran in their very blood.

I wonder where he actually comes from. Was it a place like this? A woodland realm? A fallen kingdom, lost during the rebellion? I wonder how many of them survived. I wonder if he can ever go home...

"I can feel you thinking, princess." Cassiel shot her a look from the corner of his eye, never slowing his pace. "Can you do that someplace else?"

There was a hitch in her breathing as her eyes shot guiltily to his face. Then she saw that he was smiling, and she relaxed with a deep breath.

"Sorry, this is all just...kind of surreal."

For a moment, he actually softened. For a moment, that smile actually reached his eyes. But as quickly as it had cleared, his face grew abruptly sad.

"For me, too."

The words touched a place deep inside, and her heart broke as she gazed up at him once more. A king without a kingdom. A prince without a throne.

All in the name of the Damaris flag.

That was the moment that all her questions vanished. That was the moment when the words died forever on the tip of her tongue. She had no right to ask them. She had no right to be speaking to him at all. The history books had been written. The die had been cast. And Katerina Damaris certainly had no right to wonder about this lovely fae's ancestral home.

But the world outside the castle was nothing like what she thought it would be. At every turn, there was a surprise. And all its wonders and eccentricities never ceased to amaze her.

"I don't hate you," Cassiel said quietly.

Breaking through the silence. Answering a question she couldn't bring herself to ask.

Katerina could swear her heart stopped beating as she stared up at him in surprise. It didn't look as though he was lying. But she didn't see how it could possibly be true. She tried several times to speak. She tried to understand where that kind of quiet compassion could have possibly come from.

In the end, she was at a complete loss.

"You can." Her voice was barely louder than a whisper. "I remember the look on your face when you found out I was a Damaris, but I didn't fully understand it until now. You have a right to hate me, Cass. Especially you. Especially here—"

"You can't take the blame, Katerina. And you can't take credit." His eyes softened again as they looked her up and down. "You weren't even born."

She held his eyes for only a moment, then bowed her head.

"But it was my family—"

"The same family who's hunting you down? The same family who tried to kill you?" A look of sudden comradery flashed across Cassiel's face, and his lips curved up in an ironic smile. "There's a chance the two of us have more in common than you think."

Katerina blinked. Looked at the ground. Then blinked again. Her emotional threshold had been reached. A second later, the sarcasm kicked in. She gazed up at him with wide, entreating eyes.

"Did we just become best friends?"

"Seven hells." The fae rolled his eyes and quickened his pace, shooting a look of pained exasperation towards the sky. "You mortals can be so clingy."

"Is that a yes?"

His lips twitched up in a reluctant grin. The type of grin that only Dylan had ever been able to solicit. "Yes. We're best friends. Closer than that, really. You have a special place in my heart."

Katerina nodded wisely. "That's what I thought. The signs are all there."

The fae snorted under his breath. "I mean, I'm still going to kill you..."

Katerina laughed. A welcome relief after all the stress that had been bottling up. "Don't worry, I won't take it personally."

There was a beat of silence. Followed by a much longer pause. When Cassiel finally glanced down at her, he looked surprised. As if he'd completely forgotten she was there. "What?"

She hesitated, staring back in confusion. "What, what?"

Cassiel shook his head. "You won't take *what* personally?"

Her smile faltered for a second, and a tiny frown creased her forehead. "You said you were going to kill me...I said I wouldn't take it personally."

The fae looked at her with blank, vacant eyes. "...kill you?"

A sudden chill raised the hair on the back of her neck. She opened her mouth to respond, but before she could say a word Dylan raised his hand and the entire group came to an abrupt stop.

"Hang on... just everyone wait a second."

She stared at Cassiel for a second more, then hurried up to the front of the line to see what had happened. It only took a moment to forget the entire exchange, but without seeming to realize it she circled around to Dylan's other side, putting a casual barrier between herself and the fae. Like a child who shied instinctively away from the heat of a flame.

Dylan was frowning to himself as he stared out at the trail in front of them. His arms were folded across his chest and an uncharacteristically puzzled look was troubling his handsome face.

"This doesn't make any sense," he murmured, speaking to no one in particular. "I know that we've passed this creek already...but we've been heading due north."

Katerina glanced back and forth between his eyes and the water, while Tanya shifted uneasily on her feet.

"There's also the fact that we've been walking for the last six hours, but the sun's still hanging directly above us in the sky," she ventured tentatively. "Are we going to talk about that?"

Dylan said nothing, but his frown deepened as he stared out at the trees. It was true that the forest looked exactly as it had when they'd stepped into it, half a day earlier. If Katerina didn't know better, she'd swear not a moment of time had passed at all.

"Cass?" he called quietly. "I don't..." He trailed off, staring once again at the creek. "We've seen this before, haven't we? This is the same crossing as before?"

Cassiel didn't answer. The wind picked up in the trees.

"I don't like this," Tanya murmured, one hand drifting instinctually to her blade. "I have a bad feeling about this..."

"Dylan?" Katerina took a step closer, tripping slightly as a gnarled tree branch caught on her dress. "Can we just turn back? Is it too late to go back?"

At this point, she'd be willing to risk another avalanche. Anything was better than staying here another second, in the endless sea of sunlit trees.

Dylan opened his mouth to reply but closed it a second later. His sky-blue eyes swept the woods in front of them, and his heart quickened in his chest. A feeling of intense claustrophobia was settling in quick. A kind of foreboding panic, rising swiftly to the surface.

"*Dylan.*"

Katerina reached out to grab his sleeve, but a branch caught her dress again. She looked down in surprise to see the same knotted piece of wood she'd just tripped over, tangled once more in the fabric. For a second, she didn't know what to say. It didn't make any sense.

Then the branch moved.

"DYLAN!"

He jumped around in surprise, just in time to get knocked to the forest floor. He landed hard on his back, spat up a mouthful of blood, then stared up in shock at the trees.

No longer were they shining innocently in the sun. It was as if the entire forest had come to life. As if the trees themselves had taken up arms against them. No sooner had Dylan pushed to his feet than a root popped out of the ground right behind him, wrapping tightly around his leg.

"Holy crap!" he gasped, trying desperately to keep his balance. "CASS!"

But the others were having problems of their own. Tanya leapt forward with her dagger, hacking away at the offending root, but the second the blade touched wood she flew back with a scream. A knotted branch of redwood had twisted violently in her hair. Katerina tried to grab her, but no sooner had she lifted her arm than the very ground she was standing on gave way.

She fell to her knees with a shriek, staring down in terror as she began sinking slowly into the earth. Like quicksand, the ground came up to meet her. Engulfing her feet. Creeping up her legs.

"Dylan!" she screamed again, reaching desperately for anything she could use to pull herself out. She was buried up to the thigh now. And it was climbing ever higher. "Dy—"

A sharp branch whipped across her face, cutting off her scream and filling her mouth with blood. She choked and gasped, trying desperately to pull in a breath as she sank up to her waist.

"CASS!" Dylan yelled again, still unable to free himself. Instead of being swallowed by the earth, it was as if the tree itself was trying to strangle him. Another three branches had wrapped around his body, and a fourth was snaking its way around his neck. "CASSIEL!"

It was only then the princess realized that one member of their party was suspiciously missing. It was only then she realized the forest was hardly their only problem.

Cass?

The fae was standing perfectly still. Without a shred of emotion. Without an ounce of self-awareness. Without a single indication he noticed that the world was coming to an end.

When he heard Dylan calling, he slowly lifted his head. With eyes as black as night.

Oh crap.

Katerina sucked in a quick breath, her entire body recoiling in terror as the ground continued to swallow her whole. For a moment, she was simply speechless. Then she and Dylan locked eyes.

"Still don't believe in curses?"

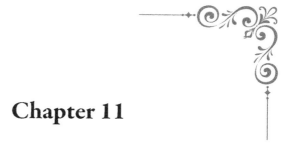

Chapter 11

"Cass?" Dylan paled in terror as his friend gazed back at him, not a trace of recognition on his face. For a moment he cocked his head, almost as though he was considering, then he swept across the forest floor, pulling out his blade as he went.

"Cass, *wait*!" Dylan scrambled back as far as the roots would let him, but it was getting increasingly difficult to move. By now, they had wrapped around his waist and both legs, with a curled hook circling slowly around his neck. "Snap out of it, man! You don't want to do this!"

But it was like the fae couldn't even hear him. He raised the blade above his head with deadly precision, hardly batting an eye as it swung back down to earth.

"CASS!"

Dylan twisted in such a way that, instead of decapitating him, as the stroke was clearly meant to, it severed the root twisting around his neck. He gulped in a huge gasp of air, then reached blindly for his own blade, bringing it up just in time to counter the other.

"Wake up!" he cried in between parries. "Cass, it's *me*! What the heck are you doing?!"

There was a sharp cry as the fae's blade stabbed deep into his shoulder. Katerina threw her body towards him, desperate to help, then let out a shrill scream as she continued sinking slowly into the forest floor. It was enveloping her cloak, her dress, creeping its way up to her neck.

It looked like the game was over.

Dylan was breathless and bleeding. Katerina was just seconds from being buried alive. But in that very moment, just when it seemed like all hope was lost, a blur of color streaked through the air.

...as Tanya Oberon threw herself onto Cassiel's back.

"You've got to rein it in, dude!" she panted, trying her best to keep out of reach as he struggled to shake her. "We've all fantasized about stabbing Dylan but do it on your own time!"

They thrashed around together, spinning in wild circles on the forest floor.

"Seriously?!" Dylan took the moment of reprieve to start slicing away at the roots still binding him. They splintered apart, one by one. "You think this is a joke?!"

"It's a defense mechanism," she hissed through gritted teeth, wrapping her arm around Cassiel's neck in a chokehold and pulling with all her might. "And you're welcome, by the way."

He wouldn't have to wait long to return the favor. The second he'd cut the last branch free, Cassiel caught hold of Tanya's arm and flipped her onto the ground. All the air rushed out of her body upon impact, and her eyes fluttered open and shut as she stared up at him. Dazed and disoriented. Paralyzed with pain. Waiting for that deadly blade of his to do its work. He'd just raised it over his head once more, when Dylan came out of nowhere, tackling him to the ground.

"Get the princess!" he shouted to Tanya, kicking the knife out of Cassiel's hand. "Get her out of here! Run and don't look back!"

Tanya picked herself up off the ground with a whimper of pain, stumbling over her own broken leg as she hobbled her way to Katerina. She reached her just as the princess' head was slipping under the roiling ground. All that remained was a single hand, stretching up desperately towards the sky. The shifter grabbed it and pulled for all her worth, leveraging her entire body against the ground until slowly, inch by inch, she began to pull the princess free.

Katerina let out a piercing scream when her head broke the surface. A second later she was dragging herself across the ground, spitting out mouthfuls of dirt and gasping for air.

But that's when the entire scene shifted dramatically.

The sound caught Cassiel's attention, and there was a sudden pause in the fight. He glanced over his shoulder, looking at her in surprise before he left Dylan abruptly behind. Swiftly closing the distance between them. His pitch-black eyes fixed squarely on her face.

That's when she realized something very important. Dylan wasn't the primary target.

She was.

Every ounce of color drained from her face as she staggered weakly to her feet. For a split second, she considered running away. Then she remembered who she was dealing with and she simply froze, staring in absolute horror at his vacant face.

She couldn't outrun him. She couldn't fight him. There was nothing to be done.

"Cass..." she whispered, "this is the curse. The queen's curse. You have to fight it."

But deep down, she knew it was no use. If he didn't recognize Dylan, he wasn't going to recognize her. And he certainly wasn't going to hesitate a moment before taking her life.

Then again, there was a certain ranger hell-bent on making sure that didn't happen.

"Kat—RUN!"

He flew across the clearing and threw himself upon Cassiel once more, taking advantage of the fae's momentary distraction to kick out his legs and send them both falling to the ground. For most anyone else the impact would have been enough to stop the fight, but Cassiel was a dangerous enemy to have. Even more so because, while he was aiming to kill, Dylan didn't want to hurt him.

"Please," he panted, "stay down."

His arms wrapped around Cassiel's chest at two strategic points, then he pulled as gently as possible. There was a sickening *crunch* and Cassiel let out a gasp of pain, bowing his head to the forest floor. A pool of blood stained his shirt as all the old wounds from the avalanche opened up once more, but while the pain must have been excruciating it wasn't enough to stop him.

With a feral cry, he pushed to his feet. His eyes still locked on Katerina. His entire body still straining to reach its target. When Dylan tried to grab him, he whirled around and broke the ranger's nose. When Katerina stumbled back in retreat, he took off in full pursuit.

That's when the paralysis broke, and she started sprinting for real.

Please, let him fall! Please, let something happen!

In hindsight, it was only thanks adrenaline that she was able to hold out as long as she was. Cassiel was fast as lightning, and moved through the trees with a natural grace. She was still battling mild oxygen deprivation and the underbrush was rising up to fight her at every step.

She let out a breathless cry as the entire forest stretched out to grab her. Latching onto her dress, whipping across her face, tangling in her long crimson hair. There was a noise behind her and she threw a panicked glance over her shoulder, to see that Cassiel was gaining fast. Dylan and Tanya were in hot pursuit, but they were fighting off the forest the same as she was, tearing their way forward as vines and branches tore and slashed at their skin.

For a moment, she thought it was all over. Then a tortured cry made her look back again.

Cassiel had stopped dead in his tracks and was clutching tightly at his shoulder. A second later, his fingers streamed over with blood. It took Katerina a beat to figure out what had happened. It took her a space to see the sharpened tent peg sticking out of his flesh.

"I'm sorry!" Dylan yelled as he raced towards him.

Whether he was apologizing to Katerina for not getting there sooner or to his best friend for impaling him with a camping implement, she didn't know. At this point she didn't care. A fleeting glance was all she needed. The next second, she was tearing once more through the trees.

The battle that raged on behind her was one for the ages, but it was one she would never see. Cassiel ripped the tent peg out of his arm and whirled around with a look of pure murder, but Dylan was armed with three more. They collided in the middle of the forest, yelling and cursing as they crashed together again and again. One trying to kill. The other trying merely to subdue.

Katerina did her best to put it from her mind. She tuned out the violence and the screaming and kept her eyes fixed on the horizon. If she stopped now, she was dead. If she kept going, she was most likely dead. But either way, she had to keep moving. It was her only chance.

The sound of light footsteps echoed suddenly over her shoulder and she spun around with a gasp of fright, only to see Tanya running full-speed behind her.

"It's okay!" she panted. "It's just me!"

It may have just been her, but it was most certainly *not* okay. How the girl was managing to sprint with a broken leg, Katerina would never know. She could only assume it was the same kind of adrenaline, but that could only sustain them for so long. Already, both girls were beginning to slow down, and the sound of the men's fight was getting closer. Time was running out.

"It's NOT going to be okay!" she gasped back. "It's the freakin' CURSE! '*And if a child of man were to ever again set foot in this forest—he would not leave it alive.*' How do we fight against that?!"

Tanya cast a quick look behind her and paled in abject fear. But when she looked forward again, her face was set with a hard determination. "Well, I see two loopholes. First of all, *she* most certainly will be leaving the forest." With a burst of speed, she rushed forward and grabbed the edge of Katerina's cloak. "And we won't be doing it on foot..."

Before Katerina could wonder what she meant the air around her exploded on all sides, and she was jerked suddenly off the ground. The reflexive scream died in her throat as she looked wildly around, trying to understand what had happened. Trying to make sense of the fact that the girl she had just been talking to had sprouted giant, birdlike wings and was lifting them both into the sky.

...right out of Cassiel's deadly hands.

"Tanya?!"

Her voice was choppy and shrill. Torn between sheer astonishment and a complete and utter breakdown. She glanced only once at the ground below them, just long enough to see Cassiel's burning eyes, before she turned her face once more towards the heavens.

The forest might have been cursed, an enchanted sunlit circle in every direction, but they were going up. Straight through the center of the bewitched trees. Towards the clear, night sky.

But that didn't mean the forest was going down without a fight.

A sharp sting sliced across Katerina's face, followed by a warm rush of blood as the branches of the nearest tree reached out to grab them. A second later a twisted vine wrapped around her ankle, dragging her back towards the earth.

"Cut it off!" Tanya cried, but she wasn't having much better luck.

The higher they flew, the harder the woods were fighting to stop them. And, judging by the shifter's fierce look of concentration and the beads of sweat running down her face, she couldn't sustain the flight much longer. Curse or not.

"I got it!" Katerina grabbed the knife out of her friend's belt and slashed wildly at the branches, doing her best to fend them off. "Just keep going!"

To Tanya's credit, she certainly tried. Her wings pumped powerfully through the air, but they were losing momentum and the trees were closing in on every side. After only a few seconds, the knife was knocked clean out of Katerina's hand. A moment later, a heavy branch struck Tanya across the back of the head. They dropped down a few feet, tilting dizzily, then another branch wrapped suddenly around the princess' waist, jerking her violently through the sky.

There was a painful gasp. Followed by a rush of air. Then all was quiet.

Time seemed to move in slow motion as she slipped from Tanya's hands. The branch disappeared, and her hair billowed up around her as she started to fall. There was a scream from somewhere in the distance, a very human scream, but she didn't know whose it was.

Then everything went black.

IT TOOK KATERINA A long time to realize she was awake. Even after her eyes were open. Even after she'd been staring at the ceiling. It took her a long time to realize her head was on a pillow, and her body was on a mattress, and she was in a *bed* for the first time in what felt like a very long time.

Things came back slowly. Lighting her brain in little flashes. Then fading back into a fog.

Get up. You need to get up.

A stabbing pain shot through her body as she tried to sit up, followed immediately after by the strangest feeling of weightlessness. Her head spun, and she threw out her arms for balance, only to realize that one of them was bandaged. Along with her wrist. Along with her foot.

What the hell?

Then, all at once, the memories came rushing back. The queen's curse. The forest coming to life. The desperate flight towards the sky, and then...falling. She couldn't remember anything past that. Just the sensation of falling, then the whole world went dark.

And I wasn't the only one...

With a painful gasp, Katerina's feet hit the floor. She looked up, only to discover that all three of her friends were lying in beds next to hers. It was morning, and they appeared to be in an infirmary of some kind. An oddly pleasant-looking room, considering the circumstances, with walls of creamy white stone that opened up to a full window overlooking a picturesque little village just beyond.

But it wasn't the *where* that concerned her. It was the *who*, the *how*, and the *why*.

After casting a frantic look around to make sure the four of them were alone, she limped hastily across the smooth stone to check on the others. Her heart froze in her chest with each one, staring down at their tranquil faces, before it slowly started beating once again.

They were alive. All of them. Battered, bloodied, and broken in more ways than one could count, but alive. The men, especially, looked somewhat worse for wear.

In his quest not to seriously injure his friend, Dylan had been deeply injured himself. There wasn't an inch of his skin that didn't bear testament to the savage attack, and even though he was lost in a deep sleep Katerina could tell he was in pain. It wasn't a good idea to fight a fae on the best of days. Let alone a fae prince. Let alone a fae prince who had been placed under an evil spell.

And on that note...

Katerina crept back to the side of Cassiel's bed, staring down at him with a suspended sort of fear. She'd gotten close enough to make sure he was still breathing, but her courage failed after that and she retreated to the others. But now was no time to be afraid. If he was truly still cursed it was better she find out as quickly as possible, so she could protect the others.

With shaking fingers, she reached out as delicately as she could and pulled back his eyelids. A wave of profound relief swept through her entire body, calming her like a drug. The bewitched obsidian was gone, and they were back to their usual sparkling brown.

Then those eyes shot right to her face, and she leapt back with a shriek.

She wasn't the only one.

Cassiel bolted straight up with a gasp, clutching at his neck with a belated sort of panic, like a part of him was still stuck in the fight. A rush of pain tightened his eyes, followed by a rush of disorientation, followed by a rush of fear as he looked around and didn't recognize his surroundings.

"Cass, just calm—"

But there was no calming down. A second later he jumped out of bed, only to realize he wasn't wearing any pants. He pulled a sheet around his waist and turned to Katerina, pale with shock, but before she could say a word to reassure him a frantic question burst from his lips.

"Where's Tanya?"

She was surprised. The entire world had fallen down around them, and the first thing he did was ask about Tanya? She stared at him for a second, still worried he might not be quite sane, then pointed quickly to the bed behind her. The bed where the beautiful shifter was still fast asleep.

Of course, she didn't stay that way for long.

"Wake up." He shook her roughly, far too roughly considering her fragile state. Katerina watched with wide eyes as her little head shook back and forth, spilling her cinnamon hair across the pillow, but before she could stop him Cassiel shook her again. "Wake up. Open your eyes."

"*Cass.*"

The princess reached out to grab his arm, but a second before she could touch him it actually worked. There was a soft hitch in breathing as Tanya's eyes fluttered open and shut. They took a second to focus before she slowly came around, gazing up at both of them in the soft light. "...you still possessed?"

Cassiel's entire face lit up with a breathtaking smile as he reached down without thinking and stroked back her hair. Considering his initial show of force, there was something profoundly delicate in the way he was handling her now, in the way he knelt tentatively beside her bed. "You're all right." The words were more to reassure himself than anyone else, but they had a remarkably soothing effect all the same. "I didn't...you're alive."

"Despite your best efforts," Tanya muttered, but she pushed up on her arms with a grin. A second later, the grin faded as she carefully examined his face. "What all do you remember?"

He froze for a moment, his beautiful face growing deathly still as he tried to search back through the haze. A second later, those sparkling eyes came up blank. "Not much. Just...pieces."

She nodded slowly. It was coming back to her the same way. In fragmented little shards. But one thing had stuck in Cassiel's memory. It didn't look like he'd ever be able to forget.

"You had wings..." he said slowly, trying to put it to words. "I was trying to—" His face tensed at the thought before clearing in pure astonishment. "...but you flew into the air."

Katerina's heart quickened as the image flashed in her mind. The way Tanya had taken flight a second before he could catch her. The way she'd risen gracefully into the air.

A strange emotion danced across Cassiel's face as he stared down at her in wonder.

"You looked like an angel."

This time, Katerina actually took a step back. Her eyebrows lifted slowly, and she bit down on her lip to restrain a smile. *Okay, is this the blood loss talking or what?*

Tanya looked just as surprised as she was, but secretly, the princess could have sworn she was also a little bit pleased. She hid it expertly, of course. Cloaking it in a heavy veil of sarcasm as she pushed up to a sitting position with a dismissive roll of her eyes. "What?" she blushed. "You can't be the only one."

Before he could answer, she swung her legs over the side of the bed and pushed lightly to her feet. Big mistake. The second she was vertical, she swayed slightly and reached back for the mattress. Cassiel leapt forward immediately to catch her. Bigger mistake. No sooner had he raised his arms than a fresh wave of blood spilled over his chest and he doubled over in pain.

"*Hell hounds!*" he cursed in surprise, staring down at his shirt. "I don't...what happened?"

The girls exchanged a quick look before rushing forward to help. Despite his fervent protests they took him by either arm, leading him slowly back to bed. With Tanya, his refusals were surprisingly reserved. With Katerina—not so much.

"For bloody sake, princess. I do not consent." He twisted away with a vicious glare, only to get hit immediately upside the head.

"Just shut up and lie down already." Katerina pushed him delicately onto the mattress, taking extra care as she propped a pillow beneath his head. "I think you've threatened us all quite enough."

It didn't matter what age they were, what social standing, or even what species. One thing was true across the board: men made the worst patients.

He opened his mouth to refuse, then another wave of pain swept over him and he relented with an adorable scowl. Folding his arms petulantly across his chest, while his body relaxed in utter relief. But while her words were meant to be teasing, they hit a little too close to home. Triggering things his subconscious had buried. Memories that had been lost in the spell.

The scowl faded, and the arms came down as bits and pieces started to come back. The transformation played out quickly on his face, like watching a nightmare come to life. For a split-second, he froze perfectly still. Then his eyes shot up to Katerina, shining with unspeakable fear.

"Dylan," he whispered. "Please tell me—"

"I'm alive," a sudden voice interrupted them. "No thanks to you."

Katerina whirled around to see Dylan leaning against the wall. Even looking like he'd been recently dropped off a cliff, the man still managed to smile. His arms were folded casually across his chest, and his eyes twinkled as they swept over the three shell-shocked friends.

"Dylan!"

Without stopping to think, Katerina launched herself across the room as fast as her bandaged leg would go and threw herself into his arms. He staggered back a step, but held onto her fiercely, burying his face in her hair with a hidden smile. A second later, the two of them staggered back again as Tanya added onto their huddle, throwing her tiny arms around the pair of them.

Even Cassiel tried to push to his feet, but at that point Dylan detached himself from the others and was quick to stop him, easing him back down with brotherly concern.

"Careful," he chided gently. "It'll be no fun screaming at you if you're already passed out from the pain..."

The two men locked eyes, and a truly indescribable look passed between them. One that encompassed all those things they'd never be able to say. The women stared on in fascination, but a second later it was like it had never happened. They were back to their usual selves once again.

"I told you the forest was cursed."

Cassiel lifted his shoulder in a would-be shrug as Dylan stared down with a cool glare.

"You *didn't* tell me you'd turn into a homicidal zombie the second we stepped inside, though."

There was a guilty pause, then the fae's eyes dropped down to the bedspread. "Yeah...that was a surprise to me, too."

A medley of both extreme amusement and exasperation flickered across Dylan's face, but before he could open his mouth to respond the door opened, and the four friends leapt back of one accord—huddled closely together as they braced themselves for whatever was to come.

Fortunately, it was nothing more than the world's friendliest doctor.

"Oh, my heavens!" He almost dropped his pen and clipboard as he stared up at them in shock. "You're awake—all of you! I didn't think that would happen for quite some time!"

"We're just full of surprises." Dylan stepped forward with a tight smile, casually shielding the others from view as he looked the doctor up and down. "I'm sorry, I don't think we've met..."

The man stared at him for a second more, remembering his manners all at once.

"Of course. You must have thousand questions." He grasped Dylan's hand without a second's pause, shaking it profusely. "My name is Tobias Matlock. I'm the resident doctor here in Vale. You were brought in late last night for treatment. Some rather serious injuries between the lot of you, but don't worry, you're all going to be just fine."

"Vale?"

Dylan pulled back in surprise. Apparently, they were much farther off course than he'd originally thought. His eyes flickered automatically out the window before returning to the doctor with an instinctual unease. It wasn't in his nature to rely upon the kindness of strangers, and he didn't quite know what to make of this one now.

Katerina, on the other hand, couldn't be more grateful.

"We really can't thank you enough." She limped forward with a smile, pushing past Dylan despite his continual efforts to shield her from view. "*All* of us," she added pointedly, elbowing him discreetly in the ribs. "If it weren't for you, there's a good chance we could have died out there."

There was an awkward beat of silence, then the others took their cue. Filling the air with half-hearted murmurs of gratitude, while taking great care to avoid the doctor's eyes. After another elbow to the ribs even Dylan joined in, though he continued to study the doctor cautiously.

"I'm sorry, but I'm having trouble understanding..." Dylan trailed off, searching the man's face for any hint of a lie. "Where exactly did you find us—"

"Perhaps I can answer that question."

The door pushed open again, and a group of five tall men strode into the infirmary. This time, the gang's reaction was much more difficult to hide. Katerina fell back into Dylan's shadow, while his hand drifted instinctively to his blade. Tanya's eyes darted swiftly to the exits, forming a dozen contingency plans on the fly, while Cassiel pushed slowly to his feet.

It was a defensive posture that didn't lessen in the slightest, even when the man in the middle stepped forward with a reassuring smile.

"Henry Chambers, acting magistrate of Vale." He wasn't exactly friendly, but at least he was courteous. And his eyes shone with open curiosity as he looked the youngsters up and down. "It was my men and I who found you on the edge of the forest; we were coming back from a hunt."

Dylan never blinked, staring at the man with a carefully practiced calm. "You hunt in Laurelwood Forest?"

It was a test. One they'd had the unfortunate experience of learning firsthand. But the man didn't falter for an instant. He appeared to be telling the truth.

"No, none of the villagers go into the forest," he replied evenly. "But we hunt in the glen that borders the northwestern edge."

"A lot of pheasants this time of year," one of the men standing behind him volunteered.

"Yes, a lot of pheasants." Henry's eyes twinkled as he continued to look the travelers up and down. "Like I said, no one goes into the forest—for the simple reason that no one who's tried has ever come back out. Which is why we were so surprised to have found the four of you."

A little chill crept up Katerina's spine, and she inched even closer to Dylan. His eyes were fixed on the man, but he said nothing. Waiting for him to make the first move.

"Rather, we found the two of you," Henry clarified, gesturing to the girls. "This one was unconscious, and *this* one," he jerked his fingers towards Katerina, "kept screaming that there were two more inside. Wouldn't let us touch her until we promised to go and look."

The princess blushed. She didn't remember any of that. But the words had a profound effect on Dylan. For the first time since the door had opened he lowered his defenses, staring at the man with something close to respect.

"And you did?" he asked, unable to keep the surprise from his voice. "You went inside?"

The man met his gaze for a moment before his face softened as well. While the gang was in their late-teens—with one immortal exception—he and his men were close to forty. It was impossible not to feel protective, even slightly paternal, at the sight of injured youngsters travelling on their own.

"You're just a kid," he said quietly before becoming abruptly gruff. "At any rate, it isn't often that we get strangers up in these parts. The last thing we'd want to be is...inhospitable."

His tone ended the discussion, at least for now. With a quick gesture of his hand, the rest of his men emptied the room. He made to follow them, pausing only to give instructions to the doctor.

"Let me know what they need, and I'll send up supplies." His eyes flickered over the blood-stained sheets before tightening around the edges. "In the meantime, make sure they get lots of rest."

At this point Cassiel and Dylan shared a quick glance, after which Dylan stepped quickly forward. A charming smile was painted across his face. One that very rarely failed to hit its mark. "Thank you for that. But it won't be necessary." He cocked his head towards the others in a seemingly casual gesture. "It's actually time we get back on the road."

Both Henry and the doctor turned to him with matching looks of amusement but said not a word. Instead, they simply watched as he stammered on, sounding less and less credible all the while.

"Seriously, we're just fine." To prove his point he clapped Cassiel cheerfully on the shoulder, ignoring the fresh wave of blood that followed. "If we could just give back our clothes—"

"You're fine, are you?" Henry's eyes twinkled as he stepped forward again, staring at the boy in front of him with growing fondness. "In that case, I wish you well."

He offered out his hand for a cordial farewell, and Dylan glanced down in surprise, pleased he was relenting so quickly. His body relaxed, and he flashed a quick smile, nodding his gratitude.

Then he made the extreme mistake of shaking the man's hand.

To start, Henry Chambers didn't shake. He pulled. And the second he did, the newly stitched hole in Dylan's shoulder reopened with a vengeance. He jerked forward with a gasp, unable to hide it, then bowed his head, refusing to meet the man's eyes.

Everyone else in the room froze as Henry gently released Dylan's hand, staring down at him in a way that convinced Katerina he had sons. After a moment's pause he cleared his throat softly, a silent demand that the young man meet his gaze.

"What's your name?"

Riley. Katerina had heard the alias before. *Riley O'Keathe.*

"Dylan."

For the second time the room froze in surprise. But Henry flashed him a genuine smile.

"Get some rest, Dylan. We'll see you for dinner tonight."

The ranger said not a word as the man swept out of the room. The doctor was soon to follow, and only a moment later the four friends were left alone. No one said anything for a moment, they merely stood there in an increasingly comical silence. Then Dylan tilted his chin with an admirable air of nonchalance and headed back to his bed.

"I decided we should stay."

It was a testament to the delicate state of his ego that none of the others said a word to contest this. They merely climbed into their own beds, hiding secret smiles all the while.

Sure. Katerina pulled the blankets up to her face, covering her mischievous grin. *You decided.*

Chapter 12

The gang didn't rest at all that day. Didn't sleep a wink. Instead, they spent every second strategizing. Mapping routes, patrolling the infirmary, and devising various methods of escape should their new hosts turn out to be less than hospitable.

At least, that was the plan. But then they accidentally fell asleep.

There was only so much abuse the human body could take. Only so much blood loss, trauma, and sheer exhaustion before it took matters into its own hands and lost consciousness. It was a full twelve hours before Katerina opened her eyes again. A full twelve hours on a mattress, with a pillow, in a heated room. Three things she half-thought she'd never experience again.

"Dylan?" she murmured automatically, pushing back her messy curls and gazing in sleepy disorientation around the room. "Are you here?"

The others were still out cold. All sprawled out in various poses of childlike fatigue on the beds. Cassiel had pulled the covers all the way over his face, Tanya had somehow twisted around herself like a pretzel, and Dylan? Well, Dylan had to be the cutest one of all.

Katerina pushed to her feet and tiptoed across the room with a little smile, gazing down at him with a feeling of tenderness she was having a hard time trying to control.

His hair was sprawled across the mattress like a messy halo, one shoe had been lost while the other was dangling from his ankle by nothing but a lace, and he was hugging a pillow to his chest like it was some kind of teddy bear, squeezing it occasionally tighter as he twitched in his sleep.

Too. Cute. For. Words.

For a moment, she simply stared. Then, without saying a word, she perched upon the edge of the mattress and brushed back a strand of his wild hair. His eyes snapped open the instant they touched, and his hand shot out to catch her wrist. She flashed a smile, then waited patiently.

Her new friends spooked easily. She was learning to adapt.

It took him a second to get his bearings before he slowly released her. He was just as thrown by their cushy surroundings as she was herself, and by the time he registered that it was beginning to grow dark outside he sat up on the mattress in alarm.

"What time is it?" His voice was scratchy, and his words were thick with sleep. Although he had yet to notice, he had not yet let go of the pillow.

The princess smiled even wider, reaching up again to run her fingers through his hair. "I think it's coming up on around seven. There's a giant clock in the town square, and you can see it from here. People are getting ready for dinner."

He nodded quickly, then registered her touch for the first time. While he instinctively tensed, he didn't pull away. Quite the contrary. His eyes flickered to hers with a curious little smile. "What's this?"

She had no idea what was making her so bold. She had no idea what was making her feel this way at all—given the living hell they'd just been through. But, for the first time in what felt like ages, she was rested, well-fed, and felt some small degree of security. It left her mind free to wander onto different things. Like the man who occasionally kissed her with no explanation.

She flashed another grin but didn't remove her hand. She rather liked touching his hair. The messy waves. The silky texture. It was the kind of hair that was just dying to be played with. "I don't know," she answered coyly, twirling a lock of it between her fingers. "Nothing."

His lips parted uncertainly, but for once the great Dylan Aires didn't know what to say. He simply sat there, staring back with a tentative smile, leaning subconsciously into her hand. They stayed that way for a long moment, and it looked like he was about to break the silence, when there was a faint rustling of sheets behind them as Cassiel unearthed himself from his nocturnal tomb.

"Seven hells." The fae stretched his arms painfully, feeling the spot where the doctor had laced a series of silver stiches through his skin. "I could use a drink."

Katerina retracted her hand immediately, and Dylan dropped his eyes with a grin. The moment was effectively ruined. But that didn't mean there wouldn't be plenty of others to come.

Hopefully.

"Dylan?"

The ranger twisted his head, glancing over with an amused smile at his friend. A friend who seemed blessed with the world's worst timing. "Yeah?"

"At some point in the woods...did you stab a tent peg through my arm?"

Katerina took that as her cue to leave. She pushed quickly to her feet, taking a step back as Dylan did the same. "You should probably—"

"Yeah, we're going to need to talk that one out."

There was an awkward moment as they both tried to walk past the other, mirroring each other's every move. Then Dylan lifted her by the shoulders and set her aside, giving her a little wink as he headed over to discuss with his friend the hazards of witchcraft and camping.

"Oh, that's fine. No one ask about how *I'm* doing."

Katerina turned around with a grin to see Tanya sitting up in the center of the bed. A small nest of blankets was circled around her, and despite the fact that they were safe, dry, and indoors for the first time in weeks, she was looking distinctly sorry for herself.

"Well good morning, sunshine." The princess perched on the edge of her bed with a little smile, wondering what could possibly be going on inside that crazy head. "Sleep well?"

"Too well," Tanya replied, stifling a shudder. "I dreamt we were all trapped in this cursed forest where I got bitch-slapped by a fern, then one of us went crazy and started trying to kill all the others." She looked up dryly as the room fell suddenly silent. "What? Too soon?"

In what turned out to be rather fortunate timing, there was a knock on the door.

"Who is it?" Dylan called warily.

No sooner had he asked the question than it pushed open and a tiny, middle-aged woman bustled inside. In her arms, there was a stack of freshly laundered clothing. Clothing that looked very familiar, despite the uncharacteristic absence of blood.

"Your clothes," she said with no preamble, setting them down on a chair. "And after you get dressed, Mr. Chambers requested the pleasure of your company at a feast in the town square. He wanted me to let you know we're having pheasant. It's already started, so no need to rush. Just come down whenever you're ready. And let me know if there's anything else you need."

She left as quickly as she'd come, leaving the gang staring blankly at the clothes. It was quiet for a moment, then Tanya turned with a hopeful smile to the others.

"So, I know we were heading to Brookfield, but I have a better idea. Let's stay here. *Forever.*"

Cassiel laughed quietly and moved forward to grab his shirt, tossing the shifter her cloak at the same time. "You have my vote. Dylan can build us a house at the edge of the village."

"Wait," Dylan slipped his leather jacket over his arms, "why do I have to build the house?"

"Because you stabbed me in the shoulder with a tent peg."

"I thought we'd gotten past that—"

"*Guys.*" Katerina stood in the center of the room, fully dressed and feeling happier than she had in a long time. She waited until all eyes were on her, then cocked her head towards the door with a little smile. "Let's go to a feast."

IT MAY NOT HAVE BEEN a 'feast' by any royal standard to which she'd become accustomed, but Katerina couldn't remember the last time she'd had so much fun. While she'd only been in exile for a little over a month, so much had happened that she'd almost forgotten what it felt like to relax, let her guard down, and simply enjoy herself in the company of good friends.

The gang ate, and drank, and laughed far into the night. The second the sun went down the villagers had lit a massive bonfire. Musicians wielding flutes, and guitars, and fiddles weaved their way seamlessly through the crowd—all chiming in with the same festive tune that looped in a continual chorus as the stars peeked down curiously through the clouds.

Henry Chambers—or just Henry, as he insisted on being called—turned out to be everything the four friends could have hoped to find in a host. He was as generous as he was engaging. As curious as he was kind. And no matter how many drinks they consumed or how late the conversation stretched into the night, he never pressed. Never asked a single question they wouldn't be able to answer. Never said or did anything to set them on guard. By the time the dinner portion of the evening was over, and the dancing had begun, Katerina looked over twice and saw Dylan laughing openly at something the man had said. No defenses. No resistance. No lies.

Considering everything they'd endured over the last few weeks, it felt like the perfect end to what had been an endlessly long day. The princess clutched her flagon of ale with both hands and leaned with a contended smile against Dylan's shoulder. Soaking in the atmosphere. Taking in every detail of the lively party. Every person. Every song. Committing them all to memory.

Vale was as unique in its remote location as it was in its diverse population. Just at a glance, the princess counted no fewer than twenty different species. All enjoying the same party. All living in a perfect state of coexistence. It was unlike anything she'd ever seen. A virtual poster for the benefits of supernatural integration. Dwarves building fires. Pixies garnishing plates. Shifters dolling out ale.

It was a living fairytale. Tucked away in the shadows of the mountains.

Of course, at every stage of the night, there had been several pairs of eyes staring right back.

The lively city rarely got any outside company, and although the magistrate might have been the model of discretion the presence of the four beautiful strangers—found along the edge of the mysterious forest—was enough to set the youthful population ablaze.

Katerina had almost forgotten what it was like to be in the company of other people their own age. The men looked at the women. The women looked at the men. But although the gang received many propositions throughout the night (some innocent, some with varying degrees of indecency), they turned down each and every one. Sticking close together at all times.

For once, it wasn't a fear-based reaction. It wasn't done in the context of watching each other's backs. Something had changed since that night after the storm. Something that had grown stronger with each passing day. A bond had been forged. The strength of which the four friends were only just becoming aware themselves.

"I'm not going to lie, Cass. I thought you'd go for her." Dylan nodded at the retreating back of a young woman who'd just asked the fae to dance. "Broken ribs or not. She was hot."

Katerina's spine stiffened, but at the same time Dylan wrapped his arm around her waist with a little wink. *He* didn't think so. He was only giving Cassiel a hard time.

But it seemed Cassiel couldn't care less. The man had an undeniable reputation with the ladies, but after a certain angelic transformation in the woods he only had eyes for one girl. A girl who had been conspicuously missing from the party for the last thirty minutes.

"Have you seen Tanya?" he asked, oblivious to the transparent timing of the words.

Katerina and Dylan exchanged a quick grin before he downed the rest of his ale. "She wandered off with a group of shifters a while ago—said she'd be right back."

The fae nodded distractedly, his eyes sweeping over the crowd before he pushed suddenly to his feet. "I'm getting another drink. You guys want one?"

"Absolutely," Dylan replied. Katerina shook her head.

The two of them watched him disappear, weaving his way through the crowd, before turning back to the fire. The musicians had struck up a slower tune now. A deliciously hypnotic melody that had the people of the village swaying in front of the flames.

"I still can't believe what happened," Katerina said quietly. Dylan glanced down curiously, and she stifled a quiet sigh. "I'm trying not to think about it. I mean, I'm trying to put it from my mind. But I still can't believe what all happened...back in the woods."

His arm tightened again as the two of them fell silent. Playing it back again and again as they stared with troubled eyes into the fire. It wasn't the kind of thing you could even begin to process. It wasn't the kind of thing where you could hope to gain the mental upper hand. You simply had to wait for it to wash over you. Bit by bit. Piece by devastating piece.

"And all because of a curse." Katerina's eyes were wide with wonder as she stared into the flames. "One woman's curse, five hundred years later—it did *all* that."

"Not just any woman," Dylan corrected gently. "A queen of the Fae. I can't imagine a worse enemy to have. There isn't a force in the world that could convince me to get in her path."

"But that's just what I don't understand." Katerina twisted around to face him. "It's easy to see why the Fae used to be in power, but how could they have ever been defeated? I've seen Cassiel fight, and he would have been just one man in an army of thousands. The power of that queen's curse? Half a millennium later? How could the five king-doms have possibly fallen?"

Dylan stared at her for a long moment, then turned back to the fire with a quiet sigh. "Your ancestors used magic. Different magic than the Fae's. Wizard magic." His voice tightened slightly at the word. "There are few things more powerful and destructive in this world. It was so powerful, that once your father ascended to the throne he killed all the wizards as well."

"All except one," Cassiel interjected.

Katerina straightened up with a flush. She hadn't heard him come back and hadn't realized he'd been listening. She probably would have saved the question for another time. But the fae didn't seem to mind. In fact, he seemed unnervingly interested as he settled down beside them, pausing only to hand Dylan a drink.

"One he kept as a slave to protect him. A royal pet." His eyes glowed with sudden intensity as they fixed on the dancing flames. "Ru-mor has it that he's still there, living in the castle."

A dreadful sinking feeling filled the pit of the princess' stomach. As if she'd swallowed a heavy stone. She'd often wondered, but never asked. Like so many things in her life.

"Alwyn," she quietly confirmed. The fae's eyes danced with a venge-ful kind of hunger, and she stiffened defensively. "The man raised me as a child, taught me everything he knew. He actually risked his life just to save mine, to get me safely out of the castle."

Cassiel nodded casually, but Katerina had a terrible feeling that if they ever finally did get back to the castle and he met Alwyn, none of that would make the slightest bit of difference.

There was a beat of awkward silence, and Dylan cleared his throat. Then a head of cinnamon hair bobbed towards them, and they breathed a collective sigh of relief. A second later, Tanya plopped down beside them. Breathless and flushed. She wasted no time in stealing Dylan's ale.

"Where have you been—"

Katerina started to ask, but Cassiel interrupted her with the far more obvious question.

"What happened to your hair?"

Together, the three of the leaned forward, staring with wide eyes. Tanya may have only been gone half an hour, but she'd come back an entirely new woman.

No longer did her silky hair fall in a shoulder-length bob, but it had been cut into a delightful array of sharp angles. The sides were shaved down incredibly short, while the top cascaded down her back in a series of jagged waves. There was no other word to describe it. It was badass.

She blushed a little under the weight of their staring but looked incredibly pleased. "I had to cut it pretty severely with my knife when I got stuck up in that tree." No matter what she did, she couldn't stop touching the sides. "One of the girls here helped me even it out."

As she spoke, Katerina had a vague recollection of her being lifted into the air with a tree branch twisting through her hair. Come to think of it, things had looked pretty rough back in the infirmary. She's written it off as sleep-deprivation and severe bed-head.

"So...what do you think?"

Tanya addressed the question to the whole group, but it was clear she was only looking for one person to answer. Cassiel's eyes swept her up and down with a twinkling smile.

"I like it."

She blushed again, running a hand nervously along the edge and trying very hard to act as though she didn't care. "I thought you preferred long nymph hair."

The fae shook his head, those bright eyes never leaving her face. "It looks nice. It suits you."

There was another awkward pause before Dylan pushed abruptly to his feet, pulling Katerina along with him. "I think we're going to...go be somewhere else."

Without another word the two of them vanished into the crowd, weaving their way, hand in hand, through the throng of dancing bodies. Katerina flitted along behind him with a grin, stealing occasional glances back over her shoulder at the two people sitting together on the bench.

"That was really smooth," she teased as soon as it was quiet enough to hear. They had left the party behind, and were walking along one of the moonlit trails that circled the edge of the city. "'*I think we're going to go be somewhere else*'? That's really the best you could do?"

"Give me a break," he grinned, stifling a theatric shudder. "I didn't want to see that."

"Why not?" Katerina circled around in front of him, pulling them both to a stop. "I think it's adorable. Although, I wouldn't have thought Tanya was really Cass' type."

Dylan rolled his eyes. "Cass doesn't really have a type beyond *woman*. But Tanya'd better be serious about it. She'd better not just be jerking him around."

The princess' eyebrows shot up in surprise. "Are you serious? You're actually worried *Cassiel* might be the one who gets hurt here? I would have said for sure it'd be the other way around."

Dylan considered it thoughtfully, then shook his head. "Cass is casual with women. That's his thing. There's nothing casual about the way he's looking at Tanya." He stuck his hands deep in his pockets, gazing back towards town. "So, she'd better be careful—that's all I'm saying."

Katerina let out a sparkling laugh, stepping deliberately in front of his gaze. "Or what?" she teased. "You're going to beat her up? Fight to avenge your slutty best friend's honor?"

"So, what if I am?" Dylan's eyes twinkled as he pulled her suddenly closer, wrapping his arms around her waist. "Someone's got to do it, and who's going to stop me? *You?*"

The conversation suddenly escalated to a whole other level as they pressed up against each other. Standing just inches away. His head leaned down, bringing them even closer still, as she stretched instinctively up on her toes.

"I could stop you," she whispered, barely breathing as her eyes flickered down to his lips. "I could stop you whenever I wanted."

"Oh, yeah?" He slipped a finger under her chin, tilting up her face to his. "...try."

Before she could say a word, before she could pull in a proper breath, they were kissing once again. His mouth closed over hers as her arms wrapped around his neck.

There was nothing tender about the way it happened this time. Nothing sweet, or shy, or soft. It was rough. And delicious. And completely overwhelming. All at the same time.

His fingers tangled fiercely in her hair as he lifted her clean off her feet, walking them both off the moonlit path and into the privacy of the trees. One they were there, he wasted absolutely no time untangling the ribbons in the back of her dress. It slipped loosely around her shoulders at the same time that she pulled off his shirt...at the same time that he pressed her up against the trunk of a tree, hitching her legs around his waist as his hands slid all the way up to her thighs.

"Is this okay?" he panted between kisses. She parted her lips to answer, and then his tongue was in her mouth, robbing her of all sense of control or reason. "I can stop—"

"No," she breathed, closing her eyes as her head fell back against the tree, "don't stop."

The night sky was spinning around them. Her hair was full of smoke. Her eyes were full of stars. For a split second, she pulled back to look at him. Then her face lit up with a radiant smile. "I think I'm falling in love with you, Dylan."

It should have been one of those perfect moments. It should have been one of the best nights of her life. Instead, a gust of cold air swept between them as she slid slowly down to her feet.

...or not?

There was really no describing the look on his face. She didn't know that anyone could fly through so many emotions so fast. First there was passion, then there was surprise, then there was a kind of longing she didn't understand. And he ended on...fear?

"Dylan?" She gazed up at him with wide eyes in the dark. The front of her dress was hanging dangerously loose, and she fought the sudden urge to cover up. "I'm sorry, should I not have..."

A flush of red hot humiliation colored her cheeks, as her eyes stung with forbidden tears. He had yet to say anything. In fact, he had yet to even move. He simply stared as if he had never really seen her before, unable to catch his breath.

The longer the silence went on, the more unbearable it became. After another moment the princess lifted her hands tentatively to his chest, feeling the pounding, uneven heartbeat below.

"I didn't mean anything by it," she whispered, too scared to take her eyes off his face. She had the strangest feeling that if she looked away, she might never see him again. "If we can just—"

He took a deliberate step back. Out of the reach of her hands.

"We should get back to the party."

Chapter 13

*I think I'm falling in love with you...
...we should get back to the party.*

Katerina was having trouble hearing anything beyond those words. She was having trouble not bursting into spontaneous tears every ten seconds as well, but that was a different story. She didn't remember the walk back to the party, only the careful barrier of distance that was between them. She didn't remember re-lacing her dress but she must have, because later she discovered that she'd cut her finger on one of the hooks. She didn't even remember what she'd said in response.

Words had failed her, but she must have nodded. Either that, or she was simply shaking so hard that he took it as an affirmative. He'd picked his shirt up off the ground, slipped it quickly over his head, then gestured awkwardly back to the road. She'd followed without a word. Floating. Numb.

It wasn't until they neared the bonfire that her senses started to come back to her. The sound of laughter and music broke through the ringing in her ears. The heat of the flames warmed her pale, frozen skin. She took a step to join the others, when he suddenly caught her by the hand.

"Katerina..."

For the first time, she realized that he looked just as lost as her. His beautiful eyes were wide and dilated, his fingers were trembling nervously against his coat, and from the way he kept glancing back down the trail it was as though he'd left a part of himself back in the forest.

The second he'd gotten the nerve to speak, he'd trailed off again. Now he was simply standing there. Quiet as a grave.

Their eyes met for a fleeting moment, a moment that seemed to last forever and was gone in the blink of an eye—then the princess turned abruptly on her heel.

"We should get back to the party."

The others were still deeply engrossed in conversation when they returned. It wasn't like they were being too obvious about it, but there was an intimacy in the way their heads bowed together under the guise of 'hearing each other over the music.' There was a little something extra in the way they smiled. Smiles that implied many, many more to come.

But they pulled apart quickly when Katerina and Dylan came back. Not so much because they were embarrassed, but because it was clear that something was wrong.

"Kat?"

Tanya sprang to her feet immediately, looping an arm around the princess' shoulder while casting a threatening look at Dylan over her back. Cassiel didn't stand but he tilted his head curiously to the side, gazing at his friend with a silent question. Dylan looked deliberately away.

"Are you okay?" Tanya asked in a hush, pulling Katerina down beside her on the bench and tilting her body in such a way that it was clear the men were not invited to the conversation. "What's wrong, what happened?"

A detached part of Katerina was surprised. The two girls had gotten quite close over the last few weeks, but not over anything like this. Not over anything normal. For a split second, she almost felt as though she was back at the castle. Talking with one of her childhood friends.

Except that I'm not. Except that those friends are dead. These people don't know me.

And I clearly don't know them at all.

"Nothing. I'm fine." Katerina wiped her face quickly, forcing an admirable smile as she reached out quickly and downed the closest flagon of ale. Tanya watched her with concern, and was about to try again, when the princess looked quickly over her shoulder and found an escape. "Mr. Chambers, this is a great party! Thank you so much for inviting us!"

Despite his insistence, 'Henry' was never going to take. The gang had been programmed with an instinctual deference to elders, and this man commanded more respect than most.

The man's eyes flickered with a quiet contentment over his subjects before turning back to the four friends with a smile. "I'm happy you decided to come. We don't get visitors very often in these parts, and I'm afraid you four have caused a bit of a stir."

As if to illustrate his point a group of giggling girls rushed past, pausing only to cast lusty stares at both Dylan and Cassiel, before vanishing quickly back into the crowd. Under the present circumstances, it couldn't have been more awkward. Dylan dropped his eyes with a quiet sigh.

"We've arranged for some rooms to be prepared for you at the village tavern for the duration of your stay," Henry continued, oblivious to the sudden shift in tone. "It's close enough to the infirmary that the doctor can continue making daily check-ups, and once some of those broken bones start to heal—"

"Actually, we're going to be leaving in the morning."

The others turned to Katerina in surprise—both at the sentiment, and at the sudden air of authority. Even Henry knew to hold his tongue. But no one was more surprised than Dylan.

"Kat," he began uncertainly, "it might be better to wait a few days—"

"It's a generous offer, but we didn't come here by chance," she interrupted briskly. "We came here for a reason—not a party—and it's time we get back on the road."

She didn't know where it was coming from. The sudden practicality. The newfound air of calm. But as the townsfolk laughed and twirled obliviously in front of the fire she found herself clinging to it with both hands. They had stayed here long enough. It was time to leave.

"But, like I said...it's a very generous offer." She stood with a gracious smile, reaching out to shake Henry's hand. "Thank you again, for everything. I really can't say it enough."

He didn't try to shame her, like he did to Dylan. He didn't even try to change her mind. A flicker of genuine respect twinkled in his eyes as he shook her hand warmly. "Now that you know where to find us, we'll expect to be seeing you again."

She smiled again, then reached for the bench to gather her up cloak. The others watched her for a moment, still trying to keep up, then pushed to their feet and followed suit. Apparently, the decision had been made. And, apparently, she was now the person who was making them.

Only Dylan remained on the fence, a look of worry flickering in his eyes. He glanced once more towards the forest, as if he could see something the others could not, before turning with a forced smile to bid farewell to their generous host.

"Thanks again," he murmured, shaking the man's hand. "I appreciate it."

Henry's eyes twinkled once more as they flashed between the ranger and the princess. The hint of a smile curved the corners of his lips, but he said not a word. "So, where are you headed?"

Katerina expected Dylan to lie. Or at least, not be so open with the truth. But it seemed the night was full of surprises for everyone.

"North," he answered automatically. "To the Black Hills."

For a second, Henry's smile froze. He glanced at the others, like there was a chance they might be joking, before turning back to Dylan with a slight frown. "The Black Hills?"

Something in his tone made Katerina pause. The others stopped what they were doing and straightened up uneasily, waiting for the other shoe to drop.

"Yeah," Dylan said cautiously, studying the man's face. "Why?"

Henry glanced between them for another moment, shaking his head in honest surprise. "Well, I'm sorry to be the one to tell you this, but a wildfire swept through the Black Hills about a week ago. Burned the whole area to the ground. There's nothing left."

Katerina didn't need to look at the others to understand the heavy significance of the words. She didn't need to hear the hushed profanities, or see the looks of despair, or watch the way Tanya hurled down her bag to know exactly what had happened, and exactly what it meant.

There was nothing left. Brookfield was gone.

"THIS IS UNBELIEVABLE!" Dylan cried. "Bloody unbelievable!"

While it had certainly seemed strange to Henry, given that their destination had recently been destroyed, the gang had chosen to leave Vale that evening. After hearing the news that their safe house had been destroyed, no one felt in the mood for a party. And, given the fact that the entire royal army was closing in from all sides, they didn't want to expose the lovely people of such a lovely town to any more danger than they already had.

Granted, that decision had left them standing in the middle of nowhere. With no place to go.

"I mean...the avalanche, the rockslide, the forest, the storm?!" Dylan threw up his hands to the sky, demanding answers when there were none to be had. "When will we catch a freakin' break?"

Tanya was just as enraged, but was keeping it to herself—furiously sharpening, then re-sharpening her blade on the edge of a stone. Cassiel had stayed very quiet—staring into the flames of their campfire, lost in troubled thought. Only Katerina was still on her feet. Standing a little off to the side as Dylan paced back and forth—ranting to the sky.

"I swear, if I'd known things would turn out this way, I would have spent more time with the witches at that damn festival. Stocking up on amulets and talismans for luck—"

"This isn't about luck," Katerina said quietly.

The others turned to her, and even Dylan stopped his pacing long enough to listen. She hadn't said a word since they'd left the village, but she'd been deep in thought. Trying to fit the pieces together. Trying to make sense in a world of chaos. She wasn't making much progress, but something about Dylan's words triggered an idea. Then illumination struck.

"You said it yourself." Her eyes danced with the light of the fire as she stared at each of them in turn. "The avalanche, the rockslide, the forest, the storm? That isn't just coincidence. That isn't just bad luck. There's intent behind it. There's a person at play."

"She's right," Cassiel said quietly. "It's like this whole journey has been cursed."

Dylan didn't say a word, reserving his judgement, but Katerina could see those same pieces start fitting together in his eyes. Every decision, every turn, every step of the way. It was too much to happen by chance. There was another person in this game. One who'd been playing all along.

"But who could do something like that?" Tanya asked in fright. She'd stopped her manic sharpening and was staring up with wide, worried eyes. "Who'd have that kind of power?"

Cassiel and Dylan exchanged a quick glance, then the ranger looked away with a sigh.

"A wizard," he said quietly. "A dark wizard. It's the only explanation."

A chill ran up Katerina's arms and she stepped closer to the fire. "But I thought you said my father had all the wizards killed. There's no one left—"

"There are some," Dylan replied bleakly. "Scattered about the five kingdoms, living in exile, living in disguise...even your father couldn't get them all."

The princess sank suddenly down beside Tanya, unable to comprehend how they'd managed to pit themselves against such a deadly foe. "But why would a dark wizard help Kailas?" she finally forced herself to ask. "In their mind, wouldn't he be the enemy?"

"Help a Damaris, to kill a Damaris?" Cassiel's lips curved up in a crooked smile, one that didn't meet his eyes. "I can think of a lot of people ready to take that deal."

She flashed him a look but kept silent. He wasn't trying to provoke her. In fact, he seemed to be the only person present who didn't instinctively cringe from the truth.

"So, what can we do?" All of that unshakable optimism had vanished, and Tanya looked as though she was afraid to even ask the question.

What could they do? Against far-flung sorcery? Against an all-powerful wizard?

For a long time, the campsite was quiet. The four friends sank into their own heads, reeling with the horror of it, trying in vain to come up with a plan. The only sound was the occasional spark or snapping of a twig as the logs collapsed slowly beneath the flames.

Then all at once, a slow smile began to spread up the side of Katerina's face.

How will we fight against an all-powerful wizard? With an all-powerful wizard of our own.

"Dylan?"

With great effort he pulled himself out of his troubled mind, lifting his head to meet her eyes. The look on her face confused him, even more so when she pushed suddenly to her feet.

"I need to find some water..."

"SO, WAIT A MINUTE," Tanya demanded, her short legs struggling to keep pace as the others swept quickly through the woods, "you're telling me that all this time, you've had a magical way of contacting any-one in the outside world...and you didn't say anything?!"

"How was I supposed to know the thing was for real?" Katerina replied, ducking quickly under a low-hanging branch. "And who exact-ly would we have wanted to be contacting?" Her eyes met Dylan's, and for a split second the two actually shared a grin. "Trinkets and talis-mans, right?"

He laughed under his breath, making his way swiftly towards the pond. "Right."

The plan was simple. Use the seeing stone. Talk to Alwyn. If there was a dark wizard out there, one who was plotting against them, he would know what to do.

Of course, not everyone had been on board.

Tanya was nervous about 'meddling with sorcery,' and Cassiel looked like he'd rather set himself on fire than put his trust in a wizard. But, at this point, they had no choice. They were out of options, and the enemy was closing in on all sides. Time to make a friend.

"Just...be careful," he said for the tenth time, standing a bit of a ways back as Dylan knelt beside the edge of the water, Katerina by his side.

"Trust me." She flashed him a reassuring smile, then pulled the stone from her pocket and dropped it into the water. "I know what I'm doing."

At once, a strange feeling of serenity washed over her. Her eyes snapped shut, and it was as though she was looking at a map. Not one she could see, but one she could feel. Her entire body warmed as she directed her thoughts to the palace. To the wizard sitting inside.

Alwyn...

There was a moment of silence. Then a voice lifted out of the water. "You called?"

Katerina's eyes snapped open with a gasp, to see the watery reflection of the wizard staring back at her. He looked exactly the way she remembered. Same speckled robe. Same crooked spectacles. Same snow-white hair—clinging like a manic cloud to the top of his rounded head.

"It worked," she breathed, hardly believing what she saw. "You're here."

The wrinkles on the wizard's face melted into an affectionate smile as he chuckled softly. "Well, not exactly, dear one. I am most certainly still back at the castle, and while I don't know where exactly you're seeing me, you and I are speaking from the bottom of my wine glass."

The princess let out a breathless laugh, then leaned closer to the water, brought to tears with a wave of homesickness that caught her completely off-guard. "I miss you."

"I miss you, too, Katy." The wind blew gentle waves across the water, and his voice thickened, as if he'd developed a sudden cold. "I can't say how glad I am to see you safe."

"But, what about you?" she asked eagerly. "What all has happened since I've been gone—"

A throat cleared quietly behind her, and she hastened to get back on point. There was no telling how long the magic of the stone would last, and there were important things to discuss.

"Actually," she amended quickly, "I haven't got much time. Alwyn; we think there's a dark wizard after us. Someone who's doing everything they can to curse our journey from afar."

"Us?" He stretched upwards, trying to see past her fiery hair. "Ah, yes, I see you've made some friends on the road."

"A wizard," Dylan interjected, bringing them back on point. "What can you tell us?"

Alwyn gazed at him curiously, then turned back to the princess, looking more and more anxious all the while. "Well, it's certainly possible," he said slowly, turning it over in his mind. "In fact, judging by your brother's mood the last few days, I'd say it was probable. If Kailas didn't know where to find you, he'd have to rely upon less conventional means. Sorcery. Magic."

Cassiel stiffened, and walked briskly away as Katerina leaned closer to the pond.

"What can we do?"

It was an impossible problem, but her old mentor had never failed her before. And no matter how much distance was between them, she had every confidence in him now.

Sure enough, Alwyn didn't disappoint.

"You leave the wizard to me." His brow furrowed with a sudden frown. "In the meantime, we need to get you somewhere safe."

"We had a place in mind," Katerina said helplessly. "But it burned down a few days ago."

The wizard considered this for a moment, poring over the vast stores of information tucked away in that wrinkled head, before looking up with sudden inspiration.

"Katy, do you remember me telling you about the Talsing Sanctuary?"

She shook her head, but Dylan leaned forward with a frown.

"Talsing—I know it. It's actually not far. But how would we—"

"You need to get there," Alwyn said urgently. "The monks will grant her safe passage. It's the only place completely out of Kailas' reach."

"*If* the monks grant her safe passage," Dylan said uncertainly. "And why would they? She's not a student; it isn't a safe house for wayward royalty—"

"They will," Alwyn interrupted with certainty. "I'll send them a message, and they will. You need to get there quickly; the longer you stay on the open road, the greater the risk."

The ranger opened his mouth to argue but closed it a second later. It might be yet another gamble, but the wizard was right. They were out of options. And they needed to get off the road.

"Katy," the ancient sorcerer leaned as close as he could to his goblet, the tip of his nose touching the surface of the wine, "just keep your head down and promise me you'll stay safe. The monks at the monastery can help you. *Let* them. Don't underestimate yourself, dear one. You have a lot to offer. You just need to find it. Inside."

A look of bewilderment rippled across the princess' face, but she nodded quickly. "I will."

Alwyn nodded quickly. "In that case, I'd better be off. If there really is a wizard working against you, as you say, then there isn't any time to—"

There was a sudden splash, and his face vanished from the pond. A second later the water grew still, and the stone floated up from the bottom into Katerina's waiting hand.

She stared at it blankly for a moment, then slipped it back into her pocket. "I guess these things come with a time limit—"

"Talsing Sanctuary," Cassiel interrupted, staring at Dylan with a very strange expression. "Is that an actual possibility? Is that somewhere *you* can go?"

He stressed the word *you* in a way that Katerina didn't understand, and she lifted her head curiously to see that the ranger had gone white as a sheet.

"I don't...I don't see that we have much choice."

"Why wouldn't you be able to go?" Katerina interjected. "What aren't you saying?"

Their eyes met for a moment before he brushed it off with a dismissive shrug.

"Nothing. Of course, I can go, and it's a good thing he said Talsing, because the sanctuary is less than a day away. We can head out in the morning—"

"Uh...guys?"

The others looked around to see Tanya staring with wide eyes into the valley. The same valley they'd just hiked out of in search of the little pond. The light of a thousand torches flickered in her eyes as the others turned slowly around to follow her gaze.

It was the royal army. Not part of it, but all of it. The whole bloody thing.

They found us.

"Maybe we should leave right now instead..."

THERE WAS NO TIME TO plan. There was no moment of deliberation. At this point, it wasn't necessary. Dylan took one look at the scene before him and backed a step away.

"We can't fight this. We need to run."

Then they were off. Sprinting up the side of the mountain. Running like they'd never run before. Flying through the trees like the hounds of hell were behind them.

...because they probably are.

In the dizzying hours that followed, the gang had only two things going for them. But they were two things that couldn't possibly be overstated. First, there was a chance that the army scouts hadn't actually seen them yet. Second, they'd had the entire day to sleep.

Just two small advantages, but they clung to them with everything they had as they raced up one ravine and leapt down another. Not bothering to cover their tracks. Not daring to cast a glance behind them. Keeping their eyes locked on the target. On the tiny mountain ledge that served as a gateway to the one place on the planet they would be safe.

The passage of time stopped making any sense in the hours that followed. Those precious moments between midnight and dawn. It flew past with breathless speed, then suddenly slowed as the four friends gave themselves entirely to the task at hand.

The fatigue was overwhelming. The pain stunned them in their tracks. It got to the point where Katerina didn't know if she was awake or dreaming. Perhaps she was in some state in between. The only thing that remained constant was their perpetual forward motion. And the fact that the little ledge was getting ever closer as the hint of dawn began to light the sky.

Of course, that's when the sound of the army grew loud behind them.

We're not going to make it, Katerina thought as the four of them tore their way up the stony mountain trail. Racing full speed to the top of the peak. *They've seen us now. They're getting close.*

It was true. No longer were her ears filled with a general hum of commotion. She could hear particular voices now. Individual people calling out to each other as the army closed in on their trail.

Not two seconds later, a wooden spear went whizzing just inches past her head.

She let out a shriek and stumbled dizzily to the side. It was the first time she'd broken pace in hours, and she felt like if she stopped moving there was a chance her body would simply shut down and she would never move again.

Fortunately, a familiar hand shot out to steady her arm.

"It's okay," Dylan panted. "I've got you."

He may have had a grip, but things were certainly not okay. As she spun back towards the ledge, Katerina caught sight of the massive horde of soldiers sprinting up behind them. Soldiers that looked better rested and better armed than she or her companions.

"Don't look back," Dylan commanded, pulling her forward with a burst of speed. "Just keep your eyes forward. We're almost there."

As shocking as it was, he was right.

They rounded a curve in the mountain, and when they came out on the other side the doors of the sanctuary were finally in sight. It was nestled tranquilly on the top of the adjacent peak, built into the very mountain. The only thing that separated them was a long bridge that stretched from one peak to the other. A bridge of planks and rope. It was swinging slightly in the breeze.

"*That?!*" Tanya yelped, ducking as a volley of arrows fired her way. "We need to cross *that*?!"

Cassiel threw her to the side as another volley fired her way. At the same time, he reached down and picked up the spear launched at Katerina. Without breaking stride, he hurled it back down the mountain. There was a swish of air, followed by a gurgling yell as it hit its target.

One down. Just fifty thousand to go.

"Dylan," Katerina gasped, throwing her entire body towards the bridge, "what if we don't make it? What are we going to—"

"We're going to make it."

Their eyes met, and he said it again.

"We're *going* to make it."

It wasn't an option. It wasn't a choice. They would make it. Or they would die trying.

The army was closing the distance between them, gaining constant ground, but only a few seconds later the gang skidded to a stop at the edge of the bridge. They stared at it for just a fraction of a second, swinging precariously over the deadly abyss, before jumping on top.

"Whoa!" Katerina threw out her arms for balance, grabbing hold of the rope. "Guys, this thing was NOT meant for more than one person at a time!"

Already, the beams were beginning to shake. The rope was beginning to tremble. For a terrifying moment, it felt as though the entire thing was about to flip over and pitch them off. Then the wind died down and it righted itself once more.

"Cass and Tanya, stay to the right," Dylan commanded, flinching to the side as a dagger whipped past his face. "Kat and I will stay to the left."

They divided quickly and did as he asked, cutting their way through the misty mountain air with as much speed as was possible. It was an impossible task but, for once, luck was on their side.

They had made it more than halfway before the first soldier set foot on the bridge.

That's when things started to get interesting...

There was a rush of air, followed by a sudden cry as an arrow whipped through the air in between them. A splash of crimson shot into the mist, and Katerina look up in horror to see Tanya's body fall precariously against the rope. She was doubled over at the waist, clutching at her side.

"Tanya—"

She started to scream, but before she could two more arrows followed suit. One lodged itself rather harmlessly in her cloak, while the other buried deep into Dylan's thigh.

His knee buckled, and he went careening towards the edge, but in a strange turn of events she leapt forward and caught him just before he slipped over the side. At the same time, Cassiel picked up Tanya and draped her across his shoulders, racing toward the doors with renewed speed.

"Are you okay?" Katerina gasped, steadying Dylan and dragging him forward all in the same motion. They were almost to the other side of the bridge, but the enemy was gaining fast. "Dylan, talk to me! Are you all right?"

He let out a gasp of pain, but when he lifted his head once more she didn't see a trace of it in his eyes. There was anger there instead. Lots of anger. And a fierce kind of determination. "Better than all right," he answered, draping a protective arm across her shoulder as they raced forward. "I just thought of a little surprise for our friends..."

Tanya and Cassiel had already reached the other side of the bridge. They banged desperately on the tall doors, but there was no response. By the time Dylan and Katerina joined them, their faces were pale with a helpless sort of panic.

"What are we going to do?" Tanya gasped, collapsing against the door as she gazed out at the advancing army. "It's not opening. What are we going to do?!"

For a moment, it seemed there was nothing left they *could* do. Then, with a smile Katerina would always remember, Dylan stepped bravely forward to face the horde.

"We're going to stall for some time."

Without a moment's pause, he reached down and ripped out the arrow that was still lodged in his leg. A torrent of blood was quick to follow, but no sooner had he grabbed the shaft than he thrust it with all his might into the center of the rope.

There was a violently snapping sound as the threaded twine gave way. The soldiers yelled with fright and skidded to a halt, but it was too late. A second later, Dylan cut the other side.

It seemed to happen in slow motion. The moment when the bridge fell.

Katerina watched with a strange sort of detachment as what had to be a thousand men plunged to their death in the endless mist, the ancient bridge twisting around them like a child's ribbon. The sounds of their screams grew quieter and quieter until, at last, all was still.

"I can't believe you just did that," Tanya said quietly, staring down into the mist.

Dylan followed her gaze for a moment, then turned deliberately back around. "I can't believe I didn't do it sooner."

Cassiel didn't say a thing. He just turned back to the door and started pounding on it with his fist. Katerina watched him for a second, feeling a bit dazed, before the weight of their predicament started to settle upon her weary shoulders. Her eyes flickered once to the mountain they were standing on, then back to the mountain on the other side. Twice, her eyes made the journey. Then a third time. Sweeping across the endless distance that separated the two peaks.

"Dylan?" she began uncertainly.

Unlike her, he didn't look. He took a deep breath and kept staring right in front of him.

"I know. We'll deal with it later." After a moment, he added, "It was the only way."

She froze a second, nodded, then turned with forced determination back to the door. At the moment, she was in absolutely no position to worry. She was in no position to do anything at all.

But the fact remained.

They'd made it to the sanctuary. Their harrowing journey was complete. The only problem?

We now have no way to leave.

THE END
Unceasing – Book 3

UNCEASING Blurb

She will fight for what is hers.

When their sanctuary suddenly becomes a prison, Katerina and the gang must work together to save not only themselves, but everyone else in the remote, alpine retreat.

Secrets are revealed and new identities are discovered as the princess delves into her past, uncovering things she never thought possible. Awakening a hidden power buried within.

The stakes have never been so high, and everyone's a target. Can the princess unlock the ancient magic in time? Can they find a way off the mountain before disaster strikes? Most importantly, in a world where everyone's out to get them...

...Who can they trust?

Be careful who you trust. Even the devil was once an angel.

The Queen's Alpha Series

Eternal
Everlasting
Unceasing
Evermore
Forever

Find W.J. May

Website:
http://www.wanitamay.yolasite.com
Facebook:
https://www.facebook.com/pages/Author-WJ-May-FAN-PAGE/141170442608149
Newsletter:
SIGN UP FOR W.J. May's Newsletter to find out about new releases, updates, cover reveals and even freebies!
http://eepurl.com/97aYf

More books by W.J. May

The Chronicles of Kerrigan

PREQUEL –

    Christmas Before the Magic

    Question the Darkness

    Into the Darkness

    Fight the Darkness

    Alone the Darkness

    Lost the Darkness

SEQUEL –

    Matter of Time

Time Piece
Second Chance
Glitch in Time
Our Time
Precious Time

Hidden Secrets Saga:
Download Seventh Mark part 1 For FREE
Book Trailer:
http://www.youtube.com/watch?v=Y-_yVYC1gvo

LIKE MOST TEENAGERS, Rouge is trying to figure out who she is and what she wants to be. With little knowledge about her past, she has questions but has never tried to find the answers. Everything changes when she befriends a strangely intoxicating family. Siblings Grace and Michael, appear to have secrets which seem connected to Rouge. Her hunch is confirmed when a horrible incident occurs at an outdoor party. Rouge may be the only one who can find the answer.

An ancient journal, a Sioghra necklace and a special mark force life-altering decisions for a girl who grew up unprepared to fight for her life or others.

All secrets have a cost and Rouge's determination to find the truth can only lead to trouble...or something even more sinister.

RADIUM HALOS - THE SENSELESS SERIES
Book 1 is FREE:

Everyone needs to be a hero at one point in their life.

The small town of Elliot Lake will never be the same again.

Caught in a sudden thunderstorm, Zoe, a high school senior from Elliot Lake, and five of her friends take shelter in an abandoned uranium mine. Over the next few days, Zoe's hearing sharpens drastically, beyond what any normal human being can detect. She tells her friends, only to learn that four others have an increased sense as well. Only Kieran, the new boy from Scotland, isn't affected.

Fashioning themselves into superheroes, the group tries to stop the strange occurrences happening in their little town. Muggings, break-ins, disappearances, and murder begin to hit too close to home. It leads the team to think someone knows about their secret - someone who wants them all dead.

An incredulous group of heroes. A traitor in the midst. Some dreams are written in blood.

Courage Runs Red
The Blood Red Series
Book 1 is FREE

WHAT IF COURAGE WAS your only option?

When Kallie lands a college interview with the city's new hot-shot police officer, she has no idea everything in her life is about to change. The detective is young, handsome and seems to have an unnatural ability to stop the increasing local crime rate. Detective Liam's particular interest in Kallie sends her heart and head stumbling over each other.

When a raging blood feud between vampires spills into her home, Kallie gets caught in the middle. Torn between love and family loyalty she must find the courage to fight what she fears the most and possibly risk everything, even if it means dying for those she loves.

Daughter of Darkness
VICTORIA
Only Death Could Stop Her Now
The Daughters of Darkness is a series of female heroines who may or
may not know each other, but all have the same father, Vlad Montour.
Victoria is a Hunter Vampire

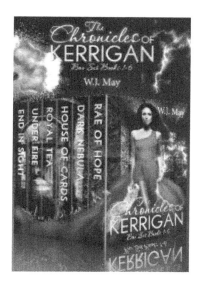

Don't miss out!

Click the button below and you can sign up to receive emails whenever W.J. May publishes a new book. There's no charge and no obligation.

https://books2read.com/r/B-A-SSF-HTXQ

BOOKS 2 READ

Connecting independent readers to independent writers.

Did you love *Everlasting*? Then you should read *The Chronicles of Kerrigan Box Set Books # 1 - 6* by W.J. May!

Join Rae Kerrigan & start an amazing adventure! By USA Today Bestseller WJ May

The Chronicles of Kerrigan BoxSet Bks#1-6

Bk 1 - Rae of Hope

How hard do you have to shake the family tree to find the truth about the past?

15 yr-old Rae Kerrigan never knew her family's history. Her mother & father died when she was young and it's only when she accepts a scholarship to the prestigious Guilder Boarding School in England that a mysterious family secret is revealed.

Will the sins of the father be the sins of the daughter?

As Rae struggles with new friends, a new school & a star-struck forbidden love, she must also face the ultimate challenge: receive a tattoo on her 16th birthday with specific powers that may bind her to an unspeakable darkness. It's up to Rae to undo the darkness in her family's past and have a ray of hope for her future.

Bk 2 - Dark Nebula

Nothing is as it seems anymore.

Leery from the horrifying incident at the end of her first year at Guilder, Rae's determined to learn more about her new tattoo. Her expectations are high, but all hopes of happiness turn into shattered dreams the moment she steps back on campus.

Lies & secrets are everywhere, and a betrayal cuts Rae deeply. Among her conflicts & enemies, it appears her father is reaching out from beyond the grave to ruin her life. With no one to trust, Rae doesn't know who to turn to for help.

Has her destiny been written? Or will she become the one thing she hates the most-her father's prodigy.

Bk 3 - House of Cards

Rae Kerrigan is 3months away from graduating from Guilder. She's now moonlighting as an operative for the Privy Council, a black ops division for British Intelligence. She's given a mentor, Jennifer, who fights like a demon.Rae finds a strange maternal bond with her. At the same time, she finds a new friend when Devon disappoints her once again.

When the Privy Council ask for her help, she finds a friend, and a link, to the Xavier Knights–another agency similar to the PCs.

Will she lose herself in the confusions of the past and present? What will it mean for her future?

Book 4 - Royal Tea

The Queen of England has requested the help of the Privy Council. Someone is trying to kill her son's fiancé. The HRH Prince plans to marry a commoner, and his bride has a secret no one knows but the Privy Council. She has a tatù. When the Privy Council turns to Rae for help, she can't possibly say no; not even when they make Devon her partner for this assignment.

Rae would rather be anywhere but with Devon, especially since she believes her mother to be alive, despite the Privy Council's assurances to the contrary. How can Rae find proof of life for her mother, come to terms with her feelings for Devon, and manage to save the Princess, all while dressed for tea?

When the enigma, the secrets and the skeletons in the closet begin to be exposed, can Rae handle the truth?

Book 5 - Under Fire

Rae Kerrigan is determined to find her mother. No amount of convincing from Devon, or the Privy Council, is going to make her believe her mother is not alive, and Rae will stop at nothing to find her.

Torn between friendship and loyalty, Rae must also choose between Luke and Devon. She can't continue to deny, or fool herself, any longer. The heart wants what the heart wants.

Book 6 - End in Sight

When life couldn't get anymore confusing, fate steps in and throws a curveball.

Also by W.J. May

Bit-Lit Series
Lost Vampire
Cost of Blood
Price of Death

Blood Red Series
Courage Runs Red
The Night Watch
Marked by Courage
Forever Night

Daughters of Darkness: Victoria's Journey
Victoria
Huntress
Coveted (A Vampire & Paranormal Romance)
Twisted

Hidden Secrets Saga

Seventh Mark - Part 1
Seventh Mark - Part 2
Marked By Destiny
Compelled
Fate's Intervention
Chosen Three
The Hidden Secrets Saga: The Complete Series

Paranormal Huntress Series
Never Look Back
Coven Master
Alpha's Permission

Prophecy Series
Only the Beginning
White Winter
Secrets of Destiny

The Chronicles of Kerrigan
Rae of Hope
Dark Nebula
House of Cards
Royal Tea
Under Fire
End in Sight
Hidden Darkness
Twisted Together
Mark of Fate

The Hidden Secrets Saga
Seventh Mark (part 1 & 2)

The Queen's Alpha Series
Eternal
Everlasting
Unceasing

The Senseless Series
Radium Halos
Radium Halos - Part 2
Nonsense

Standalone
Shadow of Doubt (Part 1 & 2)
Five Shades of Fantasy
Shadow of Doubt - Part 1
Shadow of Doubt - Part 2
Four and a Half Shades of Fantasy
Dream Fighter
What Creeps in the Night
Forest of the Forbidden
Arcane Forest: A Fantasy Anthology
Ancient Blood of the Vampire and Werewolf

Made in the USA
Monee, IL
16 October 2020